# ALL
# GOD'S
# CREATURES

## ANTHONY GARDNER

# ALL GOD'S CREATURES

Published in 2025
by Lightning
Imprint of Eye Books Ltd
29A Barrow Street
Much Wenlock
Shropshire
TF13 6EN

www.eye-books.com

ISBN: 9781785634406

Cover design by Ifan Bates

Typeset in Garamond

British Library Cataloguing in Publication Data

A catalogue record for this book is available from the British Library.

Our authorised representative in the EU for product safety is:
Logos Europe, 9 rue Nicolas Poussin, 17000, La Rochelle, France
contact@logoseurope.eu

For Anthony, Finn and Sasha

# PROLOGUE

IT WAS PAST MIDNIGHT when the Archbishop of Canterbury climbed into bed. His wife was already half asleep, rolled up in more than her fair share of the duvet.

'How did the installation go?' she murmured.

'It was very moving. I think our new bishop will do very well. But there was…an incident.'

'What sort of incident?'

'Those wretched protesters again. One of them brought a miniature Schnauzer. It bit the choirmaster halfway through the *Gloria*. There was even some kind of monkey – on a leash, thank goodness.'

'You must crack down on them.'

'That's easier said than done, darling. What do you suggest?'

There was no reply. A light snoring filled the room.

Ill at ease, the Archbishop tugged the duvet towards him and fell into a fitful sleep.

# CHAPTER 1

### i

Eastern Europe's most feared spymaster was struggling with his budget.

'How can the Paris assassination possibly have cost that much?' he demanded peevishly. 'I could have done it myself for half the price – first-class travel and a weekend with the wife at the Ritz included.'

'There were the bodyguards to be disposed of too, General. And the investigating magistrate to be squared.'

'Even so. These "miscellaneous expenses" – that'll be booze and call girls, if I know Grigorski. Where is he, by the way?'

'Just back from Turkmenistan, General. He's been overseeing the forged currency operation there.'

'Tell him I want to see him.'

The aide withdrew.

The General fingered the paperweight in front of him. A

souvenir of the Sochi Winter Olympics, it took the form of a globe with a skier who became engulfed in snowflakes when you shook it – ironic, he thought, given the amount of snow they'd had to import to make the games possible. Grigorski had been there too, in charge of hacking the phones of visiting dignitaries. The man was a pain in the neck, with deplorable personal habits, but he was undeniably versatile and efficient.

The General's eyes returned reluctantly to his spreadsheet. All those millions of roubles gone on electronic equipment and IT! In his days in the field, he had been as keen on new technology as the next man, but now it was out of control, like a monstrous fledgling constantly demanding to be fed. Yes, there was fun to be had in shutting down a city's power grid or paralysing a country's health service – but it didn't compare with the good old days of cloak and dagger. How he missed the dead-letter drops and the nights with binoculars by the Berlin Wall!

The aide returned. 'Major Grigorski, sir.'

Grigorski looked even rougher than usual, with two days' growth of stubble covering his thick jowls. His broken nose was red with sunburn, while the scar that bisected his bald patch – a memento of hand-to-hand fighting in Chechnya – was preternaturally livid. His breath had heavy hints of caried teeth and unassimilated alcohol.

'Sit down, Major. How was Turkmenistan?'

Grigorski settled his bulk uneasily into the chair, as if a stranger to furniture.

'Everything went according to plan, sir. Five hundred thousand forged notes in circulation, and a false trail leading to two top treasury officials.'

'No bodies at the bottom of the Atrek?'

'Not required this time, sir.'

'Just as well, I suppose. But always good to keep your hand in.'

'Yes, sir.'

'The old ways are best, eh?'

'No doubt about that, sir.'

'So.' The General picked up the paperweight again, turning it thoughtfully in his hands. A blizzard descended obligingly on the plastic figurine. 'I'm sending you to London.'

'London, sir? But I thought Crimea – that unfinished business…'

Grigorski's disappointment was understandable. Crimea had been his finest hour, directing Russian special forces masquerading as a local militia. Smoke and mirrors did not get any smokier.

'It can be finished later.'

'But the airliner we shot down,' he continued. 'If it comes out that the orders were issued by—'

'It won't.'

Grigorski nodded. He was a man who picked his fights carefully. There was no point in antagonising the General.

'What does the London job involve, sir?'

The General watched the last snowflakes settle. 'Gaining control of the British financial system to disrupt what is left of democracy there. Also laundering five billion dollars for the Party Chairman. And you can start by growing a proper beard.'

The death of Ben Fairweather's dog was what set the whole business in motion.

To his mind Molly, his golden retriever, was an animal without peer. Beautiful, loyal and good-tempered, she loved Ben wholeheartedly, as he loved her: throughout his twenties, she offered him the companionship that womankind had so far failed to provide. To walk with her at dawn along a riverbank rich with darting birds and rising mists was, he felt, to know the joy of the world as God first created it.

Then, at ten, she was diagnosed with bone cancer. Her decline was swift and shocking: even the prime cuts of beef that Ben fed her by hand barely aroused her interest. The vet recommended putting her down.

For a week, Ben carried her into his office in Oxford's Jericho district and watched her slumbering uneasily in her basket. Editing the magazine his great-grandfather had founded seemed of trifling importance beside the fate of his beloved pet. When at last he rang the vet's surgery to make the necessary appointment, it felt like the most appalling decision of his life. Kings of old, he reflected, had had the power of life and death over their subjects. He could think of nothing worse.

The day came all too quickly. 'It's all right,' the sympathetic nurse lied to the stricken animal as the fatal injection was prepared. Afterwards, Ben found his way uncertainly out into the daylight, dazed and heartbroken.

'You should write something about her,' said Tamsin, his

editorial assistant, as Ben stared at the photograph on his desk. 'Write something about Molly.'

'What, in *Cathedral*?'

'Yes. Something about a pet's place in creation. How they bring out the best in us. Whether we will meet them again in heaven.'

Two years out of university, Tamsin was the most recent recruit to *Cathedral*'s threadbare staff. A large, confident young woman whose colourful hair accessories would have held their own on a Christmas tree, she showed every sign of going far in journalism – if the profession survived another decade.

There had been a time when the post of editorial assistant on *Cathedral* had been much sought-after. Cadwallader Fairweather had gambled boldly in launching an ecumenical Christian magazine in the 1940s; but the scope of its features was broad, and the quality of its arts pages second to none, and before long it was spoken of in the same breath as *Horizon* and *The Spectator*. Graham Greene and Tom Wolfe had graced its summer parties; Norman Mailer was said to have snogged Simone de Beauvoir at one of them; Dylan Thomas and Aldous Huxley had almost come to blows at another. But by the time Ben and his brother Sam inherited it, the magazine had suffered two decades of decline. Selling the offices in Fleet Street and moving to Oxford had kept the creditors at bay, until an expensive website which produced less revenue than the old ads for clerical clothing plunged *Cathedral* back into the red.

The brothers had little in common. Ben, at 30, was a tall,

dark-haired figure whose gaunt good looks and thought-ful demeanour brought to mind a Left Bank intellectual in 1960s Paris; Sam, two years his junior, was a podgy, ebullient redhead who hurtled through life like a bowling ball in search of a skittle.

'We should kill the print edition,' said Sam. 'Print is dead.'

But Ben was a traditionalist who thought it bad for human-ity to spend every waking hour staring at screens.

'Over my dead body,' he said.

So Sam resigned ('I'm getting out while the going's good') and took a job in Australia.

Then, almost overnight, came the Great Awakening. Hundreds of thousands turned to God as a refuge from climate change, disease and hate-fuelled politics. Church congregations grew spectacularly; Ben thought *Cathedral*'s circulation would too. Instead, like playground bullies, the big media companies moved in, luring away his best contributors. Now he and Tamsin were writing half the magazine between them under a variety of pseudonyms.

'Would it be one for Cecil de Vere or Thomasina Campion?' he asked. 'I see them both as animal-lovers.'

'Write it as yourself,' said Tamsin. 'Make it the lead feature. It's a gift for the cover.'

Ben realised that she was right. He gazed again at Molly's photograph, searching her great, soulful eyes for inspiration. Then he began to tap at his keyboard.

Ben was pleased with his article. It began with a tribute to Molly and a moving account of the gap she had left in his life, before addressing the theological issues. Christ had spoken only of salvation for humans; Descartes had insisted that animals had no souls. Yet Isaiah promised a heaven where the wolf would dwell with the lamb – and the Pope had spoken of a 'paradise open to all of God's creatures'. C.S. Lewis, irritatingly, had hedged his bets. But, Ben asked in conclusion, 'Can we conceive of a God who blesses us with the love of animals, only to separate us from them for eternity?'

He was even more pleased with the cover, which showed two golden retrievers leading the animals into Noah's ark.

Still, no one at *Cathedral* was remotely prepared for the response the article brought.

'We've had more than two hundred emails over the weekend,' said Tamsin. 'I think we should give the entire letters page over to them.'

More was to come. Traffic on the expensive website reached an all-time high. Ben's piece was chosen by a popular digest for its 'Best of British articles' page; the Press Association syndicated it. Ben was interviewed on Radio 4, and filmed for the local TV news walking the riverbank he had trodden with Molly.

He was not altogether happy with the attention: he wondered whether he was exploiting Molly's memory for the sake of increasing circulation. But, he told himself, even this moment in the spotlight was unlikely to change *Cathedral*'s fortunes. If the magazine he loved was to vanish from the newsstands, it might as well be remembered for its celebration of his beloved dog.

## iv

Two weeks later Ben was invited to lunch at the at the Ashmolean Museum's rooftop restaurant. The email came from the Kentucky office of Dr Alex Rosewater, who professed admiration for *Cathedral* and wondered whether he might be of some assistance to it.

'Just been looking at that Uccello battle scene downstairs,' he said as they shook hands. 'Isn't it something? What magnificent horses – but how they must have suffered! It doesn't bear thinking about.'

His accent had the merest hint of a southern drawl. He was a short man with a round, youthful face and black sideparted hair, dressed in a blazer, striped tie, chinos and highly polished shoes, so that – though probably in his fifties – he gave the impression of a well-turned-out schoolboy. A small enamel badge on his lapel bore a picture of a white cat and the letters AGC.

'This is very kind of you, Dr Rosewater,' Ben said when they had ordered.

'I'd be glad if you called me Alex – everyone does. May I take the liberty of calling you Ben?'

'Certainly.'

'I like your magazine, Ben; I like it a lot. A publication that speaks to different denominations at this time of disunity – it's a fine thing. And the history! All those distinguished contributors over the years – you must be proud to have inherited such a great tradition.'

'I'm very lucky.'

'Not in my opinion. You've more than earned your place at the table. That article about the animal soul – it was a fine piece of work: well-argued, wide-ranging and profoundly moving. I'm not ashamed to say that I wept tears for your Molly.'

'Thank you.'

'Now, I expect you're wondering about this.' He tapped his lapel badge.

'A little. AGC stands for?'

'All God's Creatures. We've been operating for two years now in the US. We believe that theologians have paid too little attention to the role of animals in Our Lord's plan, and we want to set that right. An article like yours is very much a step in the right direction.

'To cut to the chase: we have some very generous donors, and some of their contributions have been earmarked for establishing a media presence. I hope you'll forgive me, Ben, if I mention that I know a little bit about *Cathedral*'s finances. They're not in great shape. That's no reflection on your editorship: it's the way things are with most magazines. I have faith in you, Ben, and I believe that, with a cash injection, *Cathedral* could really go places.

'In short, rather than throw all these funds into social

media, we would like to make a sizeable investment in *Cathedral*. We would, of course, need some shares to show for it, but you and your brother would keep a controlling stake. I'm not suggesting for a moment that All God's Creatures would interfere with editorial matters: all we ask is you keep the animal-soul debate alive. And judging from the letters you've had over the past fortnight, that shouldn't be too hard.

'To put an actual figure on it…'

He wrote a number on the back of a business card and pushed it across the table. Ben's eyes widened.

'You look happy,' said Tamsin when he got back to the office. 'Have you got an idea for the leader?'

'Yes,' said Ben. 'I rather think I have. It's going to be about guardian angels.'

# CHAPTER 2

i

THERE WAS A BROAD SMILE on Oleg Ogorodnikov's face as he wriggled into his peer's robes. In two weeks he would be introduced to the House of Lords, and he was confident of looking the part. He regretted, however, that he was not allowed a fur trim from his own sable farm: how tiresome these British were about their little regulations! After all the money he had given the party of government, they could surely have bent the rules for him.

'Very good,' he declared in a voice which, despite valiant attempts to anglicise it, carried a deep imprint of his upbringing among Moscow's criminal underclass half a century earlier.

A phone rang.

'It's Downing Street,' said his PA. 'The Prime Minister would like to speak to you.'

Hm, thought Ogorodnikov: perhaps something could be

done after all.

'Oleg!' The voice at the other end was as ingratiating as ever. 'Are you well?'

'Thank you, Prime Minister. Just one thing: for the House of Lords – this ermine…'

'Sorry, Oleg, it's not a great line. But yes, you're right – vermin everywhere. Can't be helped, I'm afraid. We spend a fortune on rat-catchers, but these old buildings… Anyway, I just wanted to give you a heads-up: the Ogorodnikov Tower is not going to get the go-ahead. Too high for the London skyline. The planning people won't allow it. Sorry, but it can't be helped.'

'The planning people!' Ogorodnikov was apoplectic. 'But you are the Prime Minister. Overrule the planning people!'

'I would if I could, but it's enshrined in law.'

'Then change the law!'

'We're doing our best. But these things take time.'

'Then I'll just have to relocate my company and build the tower somewhere else. Abu Dhabi, Singapore…'

'Be reasonable, Oleg.'

But 'reasonable' was a foreign concept to Ogorodnikov. He rang off and threw the phone back to his PA.

Too high for the London skyline! For years, governments of every hue had rubber-stamped any new skyscraper that came along; size and architectural merit had been irrelevant. Why should that stop now?

There must be an enemy at work – some rival oligarch, jealous of his success. He, Oleg, would winkle him out and eliminate him.

He could, of course, fulfil his threat and relocate. How the Prime Minister would miss his largesse! But there would be few opportunities to wear his robes in Abu Dhabi.

'The priest is here, your lordship,' said his PA.

'Send him up.'

The figure who emerged from the lift wore a black cassock with a heavy chain and crucifix across his chest. A black hat was perched on his head, and a thick black beard hid most of his face. Ogorodnikov stared, then burst out laughing.

'Major Grigorski!' he exclaimed. 'Welcome to London!'

## ii

Not since his first days as editor, four years before, had Ben climbed the stairs to *Cathedral*'s offices with such a spring in his step. Alex Rosewater's investment, he told his friends, had ushered in a new era for the magazine. Contributors who had jumped ship were returning, bruised from their experiences in the bear pit of mass media and happy to accept a generous increase in their retainers. An energetic young woman from All God's Creatures had revamped the website and taken control of the social media feeds. Advertising revenue was up, even if some of it came from strange sources, such as an animal mortuary in Oregon. Ben was able to give Tamsin her first-ever pay rise.

It was with alacrity, then, that he accepted Alex Rosewater's invitation to a second lunch.

'Looking forward to it, Ben,' said Rosewater. 'There's someone I'd like for you to meet.'

The someone was a blue-eyed, flaxen-haired woman a few years younger than Ben. So beautiful was she that, had she possessed the merest trace of warmth or humour, he might have fallen in love with her there and then. Instead he felt like an ill-starred Pygmalion, faced with a sculpture that refused to come to life.

'This is Dr Pamela Pettifer,' said Rosewater, pouring him a glass of champagne. 'We are celebrating Pammy's new appointment as lecturer in animal theology.'

Ben tried to imagine himself addressing the ice maiden as Pammy. He couldn't.

'Animal theology,' he said. 'That's a new one on me. What is it?'

'It is about to become the fastest-growing field of graduate study in the US,' said Rosewater. 'A proper definition of the Almighty's relationship with the animal kingdom is long overdue. I'm proud to say that All God's Creatures has this year endowed thirteen chairs at carefully selected American universities. We are now looking to Pammy to spread the word in Europe, starting with her fellow Brits.'

'Wow,' said Ben. 'Congratulations, Dr Pettifer. Can I ask you what led you along this path?'

'I have a bachelor's degree in sociology, a masters in marketing, and a doctorate in psychology. My thesis was on the dreams of cats. When I met Alex, this seemed like the obvious next step.'

'So you haven't actually read theology?'

'I believe in coming to things with a fresh mind. We don't want to take on board the prejudices of the past.'

'And where is your department?'

'At the University of Rickmansworth. I have just accepted my thirtieth graduate student.'

Ben was astonished. How had thirty people signed up at an obscure university to study a subject he had never heard of, taught by a woman who hadn't studied it herself?

'Now, as I told you, Ben, I'm a hands-off investor,' said Rosewater. 'I have no intention of telling you how to edit your magazine. But Pammy has some very interesting ideas for articles, and though the big media honchos would kill for them, I've asked her to give *Cathedral* first refusal. That OK by you?'

Ben didn't feel he could say no.

'Fantastic,' said Rosewood. 'Let's drink to that.'

### iii

Two weeks later, an article by Pamela Pettifer arrived in Ben's inbox. 'Time to embrace instinctivism' ran the heading.

'The Book of Genesis tells us that animals were created before man and woman,' it began. 'It is therefore clear that they have a more important role in God's plan.'

Ben read on with growing incredulity.

'On a societal level, and in the context of the space I occupy, I am a human being. But that does not mean that I should identify as one. Not the least of Darwin's errors was to claim that our species had evolved to be superior to others. The truth is that the further we have embraced the heresy of evolution, the further we have departed from God's template.'

There was more – much more – in the same vein. 'It is time for us to dispense with the old histories, geographies and hierarchies,' the article concluded, 'and partner with animals to curate a supportive and systemic empowerment principle. Those of us with agency must prioritise actions to deliver sector-by-sector change, call out faulty mechanisms and achieve instinctivism with measurable outcomes. Until then, we are barking in the dark.'

'Barking indeed,' thought Ben.

He showed the article to Sister Theodosia, the elderly Nigerian nun who edited the books pages.

'As I recall,' she said, 'there was a seventeenth-century heresy along these lines, inspired by Jan Swammerdam's *Ephemeri Vita*. Several of its members were burnt at the stake.'

'I don't think that's something we can really do with Dr Pettifer.'

'Are you sure Dr Pettifer actually exists? This reads as if it had been written by a lemur with a laptop.'

'I've met her. If she is a lemur, she was very well disguised.'

'This term 'instinctivism' is particularly puzzling. What do you think it means?'

'No idea. Tamsin, do you know?'

'Haven't the foggiest.'

Ben sat down and wrote a rejection which seemed to him a masterpiece of tact. A few minutes later his phone rang.

'You're rejecting my article. Can you explain exactly why?'

Dr Pettifer's voice was like a tray of ice cubes being poured into a deep carafe.

'Well…you never explain the title, for one thing.'

'Please don't tell me you're not familiar with instinctivism. There are more academic papers being written on it right now than on any other subject.'

'Humour me.'

Dr Pettifer sighed. 'The greatest weakness of the human race is its tendency to rationalise. Animals, on the other hand, rely on instinct, which means that they are closer to their Maker. If we are to aspire to the same state of godliness, we must stop privileging the rational and recognise the superiority of instinct.'

Ben was so astonished that he struggled to respond. 'I see… But since the Bible says that humans were created after animals as the summit of God's creation, I don't think your theory holds water.'

'The Bible was written by those who can write.'

'So you're rejecting its authority, and saying that animals are superior to humans because they're less intelligent.'

'If you want to put it crudely, yes. That is now the accepted view.'

Ben had had enough. 'Not at *Cathedral* it isn't. My rejection stands.'

He ended the call. The next day Alex Rosewater rang.

'Pammy tells me you turned down her article, Ben. I'm very disappointed.'

'If you'd read it, Alex, I think you'd understand my

position.'

'I have read it. Pammy runs everything past me.'

'Then you'll know that it's (a) incredibly badly written and (b) nonsense.'

'I have to question your editorial judgement, Ben.'

'Then we must agree to differ. Goodbye, Alex. I'm sure Pamela will find another home for her piece: one of the big media honchos is bound to snap it up.'

### iv

The *Cathedral* AGM took place the following month. Ben, Alex Rosewater, the company secretary and Mrs Prynne, a nervous-looking octogenarian who had inherited a twenty -five percent shareholding from her uncle, were the only people in attendance.

'That brings us to the end of the agenda,' said Ben at last. 'Any other business?'

'Yes,' said Alex Rosewater. 'I propose the motion that Ben Fairweather is no longer competent to edit the magazine and should be replaced forthwith.'

Ben laughed. 'This is ridiculous,' he said.

'Does anyone second this motion?' asked the company secretary.

Mrs Prynne glanced at Rosewater and put up a shaking hand. 'I do,' she said in a small voice.

'I don't know why you're wasting your time,' said Ben. 'The

two of you hold forty percent of the voting shares between you. I and my brother, whose proxy I am, hold sixty percent. Motion rejected.'

'Sorry, Ben,' said Rosewater, 'but I acquired your brother's shares yesterday. Perhaps he didn't have a chance to tell you. You're out.'

v

Ben walked home in a daze. That Sam had stabbed him in the back was not particularly surprising: the two of them had never got on. But how could his brother have betrayed the magazine their forebears had built – the magazine their father had entrusted to them?

Ben considered his own position. He had no aspirations to wealth or fame; all he had ever wanted was to earn a modest living doing his best by an institution he revered and loved. Now it had been snatched away from him when he least expected it. This, he imagined, was how Adam and Eve had felt when cast out of Eden; what Lucifer had suffered when thrown down from heaven to the infernal realm.

Over the following weeks, Tamsin acted as his eyes and ears in the *Cathedral* offices. The first development was the appointment of Pamela Pettifer as editor – or, as she preferred to be called, Chief Word Organising Officer, a term much mocked by columnists sympathetic to her predecessor.

'She hasn't a clue,' Tamsin reported. 'She didn't know what

a copy date was, or a flat plan. It's like putting a Punch-and-Judy man in charge of an ocean liner. Theodosia's been told she can't review any books that don't relate to animals, and the TV highlights are entirely devoted to pet-rescue programmes.'

Pamela's first issue was ridiculed by the media commentators. The cover was a nativity scene in which all the humans except the infant Jesus were blanked out and the sheep and oxen were given haloes. 'Animal crackers,' read the headline in one newspaper. 'Away in a manger, or away with the fairies?' read another. And yet, Tamsin told Ben, *Cathedral*'s social media following had quadrupled in the space of a week.

Ben couldn't bear to look at the magazine.

'Try and put it behind you,' he told himself. 'See this as an exciting new phase in your career.' But finding a niche outside *Cathedral* was harder than he expected. He had made the mistake of immersing himself entirely in an editor's duties, rather than using his position to raise his own profile; consequently, his name meant little to the big media honchos. The depth of his knowledge and excellence of his prose seemed irrelevant.

In despair, he turned to teaching.

# CHAPTER 3

i

A RECURRING NIGHTMARE haunted Kevin Murphy. It took him back to North London on the night of the shooting.

He hadn't been in the gang for long. Jez, the weirdo he'd met in the young offenders' institution, had lured him into it – or maybe, as Kevin preferred to think, taken pity on him. Either way, it seemed like the only avenue open to him. He had no family: hadn't since his parents' death in a car crash when he was six. None of the foster families he'd been through would want to see him now – certainly not with a conviction for receiving stolen goods (even if, as his lawyer had argued, he was too naïve to realise they were stolen). That left the room in a hostel that the social worker had found for him; but he'd had enough of rules and of the people who ran those kind of places – this one a prize nonce, by the look of him.

So when Jez said they could both kip at his, and added that he'd take Kevin to meet Big Mario and the Dapper Danz, it seemed a no-brainer.

What set the Dapper Danz apart was their appearance. Their territory was only a modest slice of Islington, but there wasn't a better turned-out gang in London. Every Saturday they could be found at Bernie's Cuts, the barber shop run by Mario's cousin, whose skill with a pair of clippers was second to none: there their undercuts and taper fades were fine-tuned and their beards teased and trimmed to perfection. Their clothes were freshly laundered and immaculate, except when business got lively. As Mario used to say, 'I don't want to see no stains on your clobber, only the other f—er's blood.'

Kevin had only ever worn what he'd been given: he could measure out his life in hand-me-down T-shirts and scuffed trainers. But to shop – or more often shop-lift – with the Dapper Danz was to enter a new world. To wear something no one else had ever worn; to open a box and rip aside the tissue paper and just smell the cleanness of a new pair of shoes – that was a sensation that thrilled him.

The Dapper Danz didn't need to steal: they made plenty of money from their drug-dealing. It went against the grain, however, to pay for something that could be had for nothing; and if they got caught…but they never got caught. Big Mario had them too well trained for that.

His qualifying adjective was well deserved. He stood six foot five in his Nike Air Vapormax trainers, and weighed eighteen stone before lunch. His hands were like baseball gloves; his collar size was the largest in the Fred Perry catalogue. His mighty frame was sustained by a diet of takeaways from the local branch of North Dakota Fried Chicken and Jewish puddings cooked by his girlfriend Sharon's mum: chocolate and pecan tarheel pie was a particular favourite, backed up by the stash of Sephardic meringues he kept in the side pocket of his blue Porsche Macan. With family, though, he stuck to pasta and *vitello tonnato*, and considered it a point of honour to take a third helping.

'You know about Alcatraz, right?' he said. 'The cooks made some of the tastiest food in America. Why? Because the governor clocked that most riots started because of bad food. He reckoned that if he kept the prisoners well fed, he wouldn't get no aggravation. And he was right: one ex-con said he used to dream of the spaghetti Bolognese. Well, that was my mum's attitude too: give the boys a good *puttanesca* and they'll behave. Which we do – with her, anyway.' And he gave a chuckle from deep within his diaphragm.

You could hear Mario coming by the music from his Porsche's sound system. Not for him the dark, monotonous grime favoured by his rivals: the rhythms and melodies of Eurodisco were what floated his boat. Baccara's *Yes Sir, I Can Boogie* was testing the speakers when he picked Kevin up in Liverpool Road that evening.

'Got some business to attend to, Kev,' he said. 'Reckon you could be useful. All part of your apprenticeship.'

Kevin climbed into the back beside Jez. Mario's brother Gino occupied the front passenger seat.

To date, 'business' had been straightforward enough. Kevin had been a delivery man, taking little packages to trusted clients: weed at first and then, once he'd proved reliable, cocaine. With the promotion had come a moped

– second-hand, but in good enough condition, with a pizza box on the back to help fool the filth. For Kevin, who had never even owned a bicycle, it was more thrilling than any of the cash Mario handed out. Accelerating down the main thoroughfares with the wind in his face, or even just winding through the back streets, he felt freedom such as he had never known before. Memories of the claustrophobic foster homes and the brutal young offenders' institution faded to nothingness.

'Gino seen this Rasta f—er down by the canal,' said Mario. 'Selling to those dopeheads in the squat. Reckon he's under-cutting us. Reckon he needs a lesson.'

They spotted the culprit on a corner a hundred yards from the squat.

'On his tod,' said Gino. 'Must be loco.'

Mario parked at the end of the street. 'Kev, you come with me. You two wait here.' He pulled on a pair of gloves.

The first thing that struck Kevin was how young the Rasta was – probably no older than himself. The second was his self-assurance.

'I'm guessing you're the Dapper Danz,' he said. 'Nice threads, man.'

'F— the threads,' said Mario. 'If you know who we are, you know you're on our patch. And we don't stand for that.'

The Rasta smiled. 'Live and let live, man. There's plenty here for both of us. Your range of weed is strictly limited; I offer more of a bespoke service. The artisan approach – that's what the customer wants today.'

Mario took a step forward. 'The f— with that,' he said.

'You're disrespecting me.'

The Rasta smiled again. 'I don't think that's possible.'

'You tell me why not, sunshine.'

'"Disrespect" is a noun, not a verb. I can *show* you disrespect, but I can't disrespect you. Check it in the dictionary.'

Kevin stiffened. There were two things you should never do with Mario, and one was to try to make him look stupid.

'You can shove your dictionary, you little f—er. Now f— off out of here and don't come back.'

'How you going to stop me, fat man?'

That was the second thing you should never do: call Mario fat. But before he could speak, three men came round the corner and ranged themselves behind the Rasta. Glancing back towards the car, Kevin saw that four more had surrounded it. A knife blade caught the evening sunlight. The Dapper Danz had walked into an ambush.

But Mario was unperturbed.

'How am I going to f—ing stop you? Like this.' And pulling a gun from his waistband, he fired at point-blank range.

'Any more of you f—ers want some of this?' he shouted as the young man fell to the pavement. But the others were already running away.

Blood. Kevin had seen plenty of it on screen: he'd watched every one of Quentin Tarantino's movies. There'd been real-life fights on a daily basis at the young offenders', with broken teeth and noses. But nothing like this – this torn-open body, the blood pumping out across the dusty pavement, dark and gleaming, oozing towards his feet as he stared at it, motionless, mesmerised.

The Porsche came tearing up the street with Gino at the wheel.

'Take this.' Mario thrust the gun into Kevin's hands. 'Stash it somewhere safe. Now scram.'

He climbed into the car; Gino hit the accelerator. A siren could already be heard in the distance. Kevin was left alone on the corner with the gun and the dead body.

Still unable to take it all in, he looked desperately about him. Then he started running for all he was worth.

In his dream, he followed the same route down to the canal, heading southwest towards the Islington Tunnel. But none of the people he'd passed that day were there now – not the dog-walkers, not the kid with the skateboard, not the young couple. The only person was the dead Rasta, running hell-for-leather after him, gradually gaining on him. And when Kevin hurled the gun into the water, it didn't sink – it skidded along the surface as if the river had frozen solid, slid towards the far bank and finally came to rest, lying there for all to see, waiting to be found.

## ii

Ben's teaching went well at first. He was taken on by a sixth-form college which had boomed since the Great Awakening, with a strong record of sending theology students to top universities. His classes were popular, and the marks attained by his pupils were high.

Then it all went wrong.

On the day in question he was discussing the parable of the Good Shepherd.

'So he left his flock,' he said, 'and searched for the lost sheep until he found it.'

There was a murmur at the back of the class. Suddenly a girl got to her feet.

'F——ing bigot,' she said.

'Yeah,' said the boy next to her. 'F——ing bigot.'

And one by one they trooped out.

When the principal summoned him the next day, Ben tried to make light of the matter.

'I seem to have lost rather more sheep than the Good Shepherd did,' he said.

The principal glared at him.

'This college promises its students a safe space,' she said. 'You have violated that.'

'In what way exactly?'

'I have had complaints from twenty students that you used the phrase "So he left his flock."'

'And what's wrong with that?'

She glared at him again.

'I suspect that you are being deliberately obtuse,' she said. 'But in case you're not, I'll spell it out for you. You put the shepherd at the beginning of the sentence. That is entirely unacceptable in this day and age. Your employment is terminated. We have no place for those who do not respect instinctivism.'

Ben rang Tamsin. 'I still don't know what she was on

about,' he said. 'Can you explain?'

'The thinking – if you can call it thinking – is that it's disrespectful to God's "prior creations" not to have them as the subject of a sentence. You should have said, "The flock stayed where it was while the shepherd went away." It's the rule at *Cathedral* as well. The subs are tearing their hair out, and Theodosia has resigned. She says she can stomach a certain amount of heresy, but not the misappropriation of the English language.'

'And what about you, Tamsin?'

'I'm looking around for another job, but there's not much out there; I guess I'll just have to carry on. But it's depressing to see the magazine so diminished.'

'My father used to say that it takes an army of journalists to make a great magazine, and just one bad general to ruin it.'

'Well, Dr Pettifer is a case in point.'

'Is that what you call her?'

'We all have to. She insists on it.'

Ben shook his head. He'd never known a magazine where the staff were not on first-name terms with the editor. Curiouser and curiouser.

Back at his flat, he sat down at the piano. It was the same one he had played at *Cathedral*'s Christmas parties when he was just a boy. The magazine had really felt like a family back then, his parents leading the carol-singing and Sister Theodosia belting out Gershwin and Cole Porter. He launched into 'I Got Plenty Of Nothing', but found after a single verse that he hadn't the heart for it.

On top of the piano was a photo of Molly. How he had

missed her and her gift of understanding – the sympathy in those great, beautiful eyes! And how much trouble his grief for her had caused!

His thoughts returned to the problem of employment. He had some savings to tide him over, but they wouldn't last for ever. He decided to ring his godfather.


### iii

The choice of Hughie Blythe as Ben's godfather had been much argued over by George and Alice Fairweather.

'The candles on the altar will blow out the moment he walks into the church,' said Alice, appalled.

But her husband was insistent. He conceded that Hughie's reputation was lamentable: he was a Lothario, a gambler and a reformed alcoholic only in the sense that his spectacular binges occasionally gave way to periods of abstinence. But whatever his failings, there was nothing he wouldn't do for a friend in trouble: he had once personally resprayed and beaten the dents out of a borrowed car after George had crashed it on a student spree. Ben, George argued, should have a worldly, practical godparent looking out for him as well as some more spiritual ones.

It proved a wise decision. Hughie was not given to remembering birthdays, but he had a way of being there at moments of crisis, and his advice was generally sound: 'Do as I say, not as I do' was his motto. Since the death of Ben's father and mother, he had become a precious link to them and their generation.

'Come and see me at work,' he said when Ben phoned him. 'It'll do you good to see the demi-monde in action.'

'Work' was Chicane, a London nightclub which occupied the basement of a large townhouse behind the Ritz. It took its name from the former owner's obsession with motor-racing; photographs of Formula 1 heroes decorated the walls, while the nose of a championship-winning Ferrari projected from behind the bar, as if the driver had taken a wrong turn at Silverstone and failed to apply the brakes as he approached Piccadilly.

'It's all a bit behind the times,' said Hughie. 'Trading on past glories is the kiss of death to a nightclub. My job is to rev it up, to coin a phrase, and we're making quite good progress. Champagne?'

Grey-haired and overweight as he was, Hughie's qualities as a heartbreaker were still discernible. His features remained handsome; his eyes remained bright; he exuded charm and bonhomie. The troubles of the world fled before his deep, generous laugh.

His career had been chequered, to say the least. He had tried the army, but had been thrown out for some long-forgotten misdemeanour. He had followed the hippie trail to India, where he had failed to find enlightenment and developed a taste for opium. A sizeable inheritance had allowed him to live the life of a playboy for a while, with powerboating as a recurring motif; his action-man persona had even led to suggestions that he was a spy. When the money ran out, he became a ski instructor in winter and a tennis coach in summer, with all the opportunities for intense liaisons that these roles afforded. Then his knees began to feel the strain, so he moved into hotel PR and later into management. The Caribbean became his stamping ground, and there he finally embarked on marriage. Marie-Christine, a former Miss St Lucia, was as intelligent and strong-minded as she was glamorous, and was generally considered able to keep Hughie on the straight and narrow. Why they were currently living four thousand miles apart was not something Ben felt he could ask.

'I know the type,' said Hughie when Ben described Pamela Pettifer. 'Second-rate academics who spend their lives coming up with new things to complain about.'

'How do you know the type?'

'At my lowest ebb I shared a squat in Stoke Newington with some of them. Two at least went on to become professors of weird isms at obscure universities.'

'Well, Pamela Pettifer may be second rate, but she's sitting in my chair at *Cathedral*.'

'Aren't there any other magazines you could edit?'

'A few, yes. But those jobs come up once in a blue moon. And in the meantime I have a mortgage to pay.'

'I don't suppose you'd like to come and work for me?'

'What – here?'

'Exactly. I happen to be short of a cocktail pianist. I assume you're still playing.'

'Well, yes.'

'Then that's all settled.'

'Armed police! Stay where you are!'

These were always the weirdest nightmares, Kevin thought
– the ones in which you dreamt about waking up but didn't.
And never had he had a more terrifying awakening than on
the morning of the raid on Jez's flat.

It had been just like on the telly – the police grotesquely
inhuman in their black body armour, guns at the ready, forcing
him to the ground and handcuffing him. What happened
next was a blur as they dragged him downstairs and threw
him into the back of a van. His memories only became clear
again when it got to the interrogation: bare room; good cop,
bad cop, one a man, the other a woman; ineffectual solicitor.

'You're in it so deep you could never breathe fresh air
again,' said the male detective. 'You saved us a lot of trouble,
throwing the gun into the canal. It was barely an hour's work
for the divers to find it: sitting right in a shopping trolley as
if you'd just bought it from Sainsbury's. Ballistics have confirmed that it was the one that killed Dwayne Barrett. And
whose fingerprints are on it? Yours – only yours.

'So you're looking at a life sentence for murder, sonny:
that's the law. Don't think the judge is going to say, "He's
only a teenager, I'll give him a break and just make it twenty
years." The judge has to follow the guidelines, whether he
likes it or not.

'Think about that time you spent in the young offenders'.
Multiply it by forty. And believe me, that was a picnic com-
pared to grown-up prison. There'll be plenty there to give you

a warm welcome – older, bigger blokes who'll like the look of a pretty boy like you.

'Let's say you get lucky: parole when you're forty. Who's going to want you then – an old man who's spent half his life behind bars? Do you think a woman will look at you – even a woman who's as old as you are? And who's going to give you a job? You'll be back in the slammer before you know it. You'll die in jail without ever having lived.'

'But I didn't do it!' Kevin protested. 'I never shot him. I just got given the gun by—'

'By who, Kevin?'

But Kevin said nothing. No way was he going to grass on Big Mario: he didn't want to end up bleeding his life out on a pavement like the Rasta. Anyway, the Dapper Danz were his family now. You didn't rat on your family.

'It's up to you, Kevin. You can keep shtum and take the rap if you want to. Or you can tell us exactly what happened and we'll do what we can to help you. Think about it.'

They left him for three hours. Then it was the woman detective's turn.

'What are you doing, Kevin?' she said. 'I don't believe you pulled that trigger – why would you? I bet you'd never touched a gun before in your life. But yours are the only fingerprints on it. All the evidence is against you.

'Do you know what I think? I think you're keeping your mouth shut to protect people who don't deserve your loyalty. People who set you up.

'It was Big Mario, wasn't it, Kevin? Believe me, you're not the only one he's used as a patsy. Either he wiped the gun clean, or he was wearing gloves; then he handed it to you, so that if anyone was going to be in the frame, it was Kevin Murphy. You were the newest member of the gang, you were the youngest, you were the most expendable. You can rot in jail for the rest of your life for all he cares.

'Just come clean, Kevin. We can help you – we really can. Think about it.'

He thought about it. He thought in particular about the gloves – so out of place on a warm summer evening. Mario wasn't ever going to warn the Rasta off: he was always going to kill him. And he was always going to hand the gun to Kevin.

'They'd kill me,' he said when the woman detective came back.

'They'd have to find you first – and we can make sure they never do. We can put you in a witness-protection programme. New name, new identity, new place to live, a long, long way away. It'd be easier for you than most, with no family ties to bring you back here. You could have a new start – make something of your life, instead of carrying on down the rat-infested sewer you're in now. You'd have to earn it, though.'

'How?'

'Tell us everything you know about the murder – and the Dapper Danz. How they bring the drugs in, where they stash them, who their contacts are, who they supply. And you'd have to give evidence at the trial. Then you can vanish without a trace.'

And that was how Kevin found himself waking up to the sound of seagulls.

It took Ben several weeks to fathom the subtleties of Chicane. It was a club that catered – with more success than might have been expected – for three fundamentally different clienteles. The bar and dance floor were designed for young technocrats earning more money than they knew what to do with – 'Chic geeks', in Hughie's terminology. The state-of-the-art laser display had been his biggest investment, with rods of light shooting over the dancers' heads and between the mirrored walls with the energy of the Hadron Collider.

'They love it,' he said. 'The DJ has a gizmo that generates incredibly complicated equations and beams them onto the ceiling. The geeks have to try and solve them before they disappear – first one to succeed gets a bottle of bubbly.'

The dining-room was more sedate, taking its inspiration from country houses of the 1950s and calculated to appeal to middle-aged punters with inherited wealth.

'I got a psychologist pal in as a consultant,' said Hughie. 'He had this theory that most of the upper crust struggle with feelings of abandonment, partly because they were sent to boarding school, but also because their parents used to disappear off to glamorous dinners every night. He argued that if we could put our members in the kind of environment where they could imagine their ma and pa at the next table, we could heal their psyches and relieve them of their cash at the same time. I'm glad to say that it seems to be working. That's your piano, by the way.' He pointed to a Bechstein in the corner. 'Nothing like a chap in a white dinner jacket tickling the ivories to kindle a bit of romance.'

Finally, there were the private dining-rooms, each an extravaganza of pink marble, gilt and Versace fabrics.

'Vulgar meets Volga,' said Hughie. 'They're block-booked by Russians. And here is the person who stops them degenerating into the last days of Pompeii. Svetlana, I want you to meet Ben, our newest recruit.'

Svetlana was tall, improbably blonde and groomed to within an inch of her life. Her vermilion nails were a work of art in themselves; her eyelashes could have been the subject of a thesis. She wore a short black cocktail dress with high-heeled shoes that added to her already impressive stature. She was the most glamorous person Ben had ever met.

'Hello,' she said.

To his surprise, her voice was not a husky Slavic drawl, but an advertisement for received-pronunciation English.

'I hope,' she said, 'that Hughie isn't slandering the clientele again.'

'Not in a million years,' said Hughie. 'Do you mind if I leave you two together for a moment? I need to talk to the sous-chef about the Great Soufflé Disaster.'

Alone with Svetlana, Ben felt like a rodent left to make small talk with a python. Most of the women in his life had been bluestockings with little time for manicures and high fashion. He wondered what Sister Theodosia would make of the company into which he had fallen.

'What's the Great Soufflé Disaster?' he asked.

'One of our members wanted to propose to his girlfriend. She always orders chocolate soufflé when she comes here, so he had the idea of asking the chef to hide a ring inside the dish. It was supposed to be wrapped in a little greaseproof package, but for some reason that didn't happen. The result, of course, was that she swallowed it. Pavé-set diamonds by Van Cleef & Arpels too.'

'What's it like working here?'

'Exhausting, but fun. The members aren't nearly as bad as Hughie likes to pretend. We get the odd gangster in, but most of my Russians are perfectly nice. Part of my job is to make sure they know the rules: no call-girls, no drugs, no guns. Once that's established, it's fine.'

'You're not Russian yourself?'

'It's rather mixed-up: Russia, Poland, Kazakhstan, Ukraine – my ancestors came from all over. My great-grandparents were both teenagers living in Moscow at the time of the Bolshevik Revolution; their families fled to Paris with a lot of the White Russians, and when they married they moved over here. My father had an entirely English upbringing, but he was keen to rediscover his roots, so in my childhood there was a lot of to-ing and fro-ing. What about you?'

'Boringly English, I'm afraid.'

'Boring is fine. Boredom is one of those rare things that is both a sin and a virtue: a sin, in that it's a symptom of our fallen state, and a virtue in that it – just as much as necessity – is the mother of invention.'

'You've obviously given it a lot of thought.'

'I have, actually. In fact I did a study of it at uni.'

'What were you studying?'

'Philosophy, plus a bit of theology.'

'So, if you don't mind me asking, how did you end up working here?'

'I didn't fancy academia – too claustrophobic. And I was too fond of nightclubs to become a nun. So I chose the nightclubs. How about you?'

'It's a long story.'

Hughie reappeared, looking anxious.

'The chef's gone AWOL. Maybe I was too tough on him after the Great Meringue Disaster and he couldn't face another dressing down. How's your cooking, Ben? Your father was always handy in the kitchen.'

'Not bad.'

'Great. Follow me!'

## vi

Clare Longridge seldom took a late train home from London, mainly because she hated driving in the dark. Her house was only a few miles from the small country station, along a quiet road, but her eyesight was not what it had been, and she dreaded meeting another car or running over a nocturnal animal. This evening's invitation, however, was one she could hardly have refused, and in any case would not have wanted to. Will Harvey had been a splendid head of chambers – always 'supportive', to use the ghastly modern cliché – and she was touched to be included in his farewell dinner. She did not miss her days in court, but she missed the company of her fellow barristers, and the occasion had been a delightful one, full of jokes and hilarious anecdotes. As the train drew into her stop, she chuckled again at the story of the junior clerk and the Lord Chancellor's cockatoo.

Only one other passenger disembarked – a man in a leather jacket whom she didn't recognise, and who strode off purposefully across the car park. Clare pointed her key towards her little Fiat, and was rewarded by the friendly winking of its lights. Nevertheless, she felt a sense of foreboding as she climbed into the chilly interior. She wished she'd stayed at her club for the night; but the gardeners were coming first thing in the morning, and she didn't want them hacking at a favourite shrub in her absence.

There was no sign of life as she turned cautiously onto the road. She switched on the radio for comfort, and was pleased to hear the opening of a Schubert piano sonata. But she still sat rigidly at the wheel, staring anxiously at the tarmac and the ghostly hedgerows revealed by her headlights.

Not until a mile from her home was there any other traffic. A dazzle of light in her mirror told her that someone had picked up the road at Turner's Cross. She prayed that it wasn't a speed king who would try to overtake her on the stretch of drystone wall. Fortunately the light kept a respectful distance.

As always, she indicated well before reaching her gate. It was set only slightly back, so the rear of her car projected into the road when she stopped to open it. There was still ample room, however, for a large van to get by. She undid her safety belt as she waited for it to pass.

But the van following her this evening was not interested in getting by, choosing instead to accelerate as Clare's car came to a halt. With the ease, it seemed, of long practice, it struck the Fiat a glancing blow, ramming it into the stone gatepost. The van halted a short way down the road, and the driver hurried back to make sure that Clare Longridge was dead. Satisfied that she was, he climbed back into his seat and drove away.

# CHAPTER 4

i

LIFE AT CHICANE PROVED so agreeable that, within a few weeks, Ben's previous existence seemed like a once-favourite novel relegated to a top shelf. His new colleagues were friendly and endlessly entertaining; between them they had visited almost every corner of the globe, and dabbled in almost every profession, legal or illegal. He got on particularly well with the Egyptian maître d', whose hobby was falconry. 'A lot like my job, Ben,' he explained: 'You got to keep an eye on everyone's trajectory, know what makes them feel at home, feed them promptly. Just wish I could put a hood on one or two of the members.'

Ben's body clock adjusted surprisingly easily to a nocturnal lifestyle. Hughie had given him the use of a studio flat attached to the club, so he could fall into bed at the end of the evening. On his days off – Sunday and Monday – he returned home to Oxford. Only when he passed the street containing *Cathedral*'s office did his old life come back to him with a sharp pang.

It was after one of these breaks that he returned to find the club pulsing with extraordinary energy.

'What's going on?' he asked Svetlana.

'One of my Russians has booked all three private dining-rooms for this evening. You might have heard of him – Oleg Ogorodnikov.'

'Hasn't he just been made a peer?'

'That's the one. This is a celebration for sixty of his closest friends. And nobody spends more money here than he does – so everything needs to go like clockwork.'

Brian the bouncer was particularly excited by Ogorodnikov's visit. His admiration for the oligarch's bodyguards knew no bounds.

'They're the business, Ben, believe me – ex-special forces. One of them showed me his kit: those curly wires coming out of their ears are the tip of the iceberg. A wall of steel, they are.'

Hughie was looking unusually harassed. 'That bloody sommelier! I told him to check the Dom Perignon stocks. Ogorodnikov won't drink anything else, and we're down to our last five magnums. Thank God I took a look in the cellar myself.'

'Anything special I need to know?'

'Ogorodnikov's favourite tune is "My Favourite Things". The moment he appears, you launch into that.'

'How will I know when he's here? I can't see that much of the room when I'm at the keyboard.'

'Oh, you'll know – don't worry about that.'

Hughie was right.

The arrival of Ogorodnikov's entourage was like that of a steam-age locomotive. First came a bodyguard, scanning the room with all the professionalism that had so impressed Brian – a diesel engine of a man, given a veneer of humanity by his dark suit, white shirt and black tie. There followed, two by two, a long procession of couples, consisting chiefly of very stout, balding men accompanied by very thin young women whose grooming was on a par with Svetlana's. An exception was a Cabinet minister squiring his determinedly dowdy wife; another was a lithe international footballer with a daytime TV star on his arm. Such was the volume of chatter that Ben saw little point in attempting 'My Favourite Things'; but at a glance from Hughie he banged it out as loudly as he could.

The sight of Ogorodnikov himself – as stout and balding as any of his entourage – momentarily stilled his fingers. The oligarch was wearing not only the full robes of a peer of the realm, but a coronet brilliant with gemstones. He surveyed the club with an enormous grin; a series of guffaws gurgled up from his chest.

'Champagne for everyone!' he commanded. 'Champagne!'

'The Dom Perignon, sir?'

'Of course the Dom Perignon! Is there another champagne?'

The diners applauded his gesture. All except one.

She was standing a few feet away from Ben: a petite woman of about his own age with a mass of curly black hair tied back

53

with a colourful bandana which gave her, by Chicane's standards, a wildly Bohemian air. As Ogorodnikov approached she got suddenly to her feet, seized the plate in front of her – laden with the chef's signature dish, a spicy boeuf Stroganoff – and hurled it at the oligarch's head.

Perhaps because of her height, the plate fell short. Instead, it collided with the broad white shirtfront of a second bodyguard.

The scene that followed was one that Ben only later managed to piece together. Ogorodnikov was about to burst into a terrifying rage when a few well-chosen words from Svetlana set him guffawing instead; the Egyptian maître d', with equal presence of mind, blocked the furious bodyguard's path with the cheese trolley. Ben himself – following goodness knows what instinct – grabbed the young woman and bundled her through the fire exit, down a passageway and into the safety of a bin-lined yard behind the kitchens.

'You live dangerously,' he said when they had both caught their breath. 'What the hell was that all about?'

'That,' she said, 'was about Durden Hall. Have you heard of it?'

'I can't say I have.'

'It was an exquisite Tudor building in Chelsea with brickwork to die for. Ogorodnikov owned the house next to it, and wanted the hall too, but the trust to which it belonged told him to take a hike. So what did he do? He got permission – through wholesale bribery – to build a three-storey basement under his house. Surprise, surprise, Durden Hall's foundations were so badly damaged that it was left in danger of collapse. The trustees tried to make Ogorodnikov cough up for repairs, but they couldn't afford the lawyers he could. A few more brown envelopes and the building was condemned as unsafe. Ogorodnikov bought it at – to coin a phrase – a knockdown price, demolished it and built a new wing onto his house, which he then sold for one of the highest prices ever realised by a private residence in London. I'd say that deserves a boeuf Stroganoffing, wouldn't you?'

Ben had to admit that it did. 'But how come there wasn't a huge public outcry?'

'Ogorodnikov started out in social media and made millions from a dating app for bikers called Vronsky Vroomsky. There's nothing he doesn't know about disseminating fake news and hacking critical websites. Anyone who tried to report on the Durden Hall scandal suddenly found that their laptop contained more viruses than Porton Down.'

'And why does it all mean so much to you?'

'Because I was one of them. I worked for an online magazine called *Architectural History Today*. Its website was annihilated, and my journalistic career went into freefall.'

'Then we have something in common.'

He gave a brief account of his progress from *Cathedral* to Chicane. 'Talking of which, I'd better get back to the piano, or I won't have a job here either. What will you do now? I don't know how welcome you'd be in the dining-room.'

'Let's see – here's a text from my date: "I have never been so embarrassed in my life." So no, not welcome. Is there another way out of here?'

'That alleyway leads to St James's.'

'Then I think I'll head home and drown my sorrows in a cup of cocoa.'

'You could always try Vronsky Vroomsky.'

She laughed. 'I don't think I'm that desperate. But thank you – and thank you for saving my neck.'

With a small wave she disappeared down the alley.

## ii

Kevin closed the front door behind him and headed down the hill towards the gallery. It was a windy morning, with great grey clouds scudding across the bay. But that first glimpse of the sea always lifted his heart, and the wide reach of the beach always seemed a miracle. He had never been taken to the seaside when he was growing up; had seldom, in fact, left the city. Now that he had discovered Cornwall, he felt no inclination to live anywhere else.

There were no surfers in the water, which didn't surprise him. It was a peculiarity of the place that whenever the thunderous white rollers came sweeping in from the Atlantic – the kind of waves, he imagined, that surfers lived for – there was not a board to be seen. On calm days, though, the beach was thronged with figures in wetsuits, paddling out and then staring expectantly at the horizon as they bobbed up and down, waiting for a wave that would carry them right to the beach – a wave that never came. A philosopher might have taken it to be a metaphor for the human condition. To Kevin, it just seemed a proper waste of time.

Reaching the bottom of the hill, he followed the road along the seafront. There were few people out yet apart from the dog walkers; the doors of the Lyle Gallery wouldn't open for another hour. Most of the holidaymakers would be having a leisurely breakfast – or, if this was their leaving day, packing frantically to meet their rental company's ten o'clock deadline.

He waved to the manageress of the restaurant where he'd worked for a few weeks in the summer. That had been a crazy time: the town stiff with tourists, every place to eat out booked weeks in advance, staff like gold dust. She'd wanted him to wait tables, but it had seemed a step too far: all those people coming through, you could never quite be sure…so he'd dug his heels in and said he hadn't the confidence, he'd only do kitchen work, even though it was as hot as hell down there. He'd enjoyed the camaraderie, and made a couple of friends – his first in St Ives.

How much better it would have been if the police had put him here right away! First there'd been five months in Norwich: 'Wherever you end up, people can't know that you're from London,' the witness protection officer had told him. 'So you've go to get to know this town as if you've lived here for years.'

That had been easier said than done. To begin with he'd been too scared to walk the streets in daylight, so his impressions of the city had been a nocturnal parade of street lamps, tail lights and looming silhouettes. There had been advantages to that, of course: if you could find your way around a city in the dark, you could answer pretty much any question about its geography. But what a lonely existence it had been! He found himself missing the Dapper Danz, even though he knew they'd kill him if they could. The witness protection officer had impressed on him that he could have no contact whatsoever with anyone from his previous life – not even a text or a phone call. She came by to see him from time to time in the flat they'd found for him.

'Sorry it isn't more comfortable,' she said. 'But we can't have you living in the lap of luxury. If we did, people would claim that you'd been bribed to give evidence.'

She asked if there was anything he especially wanted or needed, and he mentioned drawing paper and pencils. Art was the one subject he'd enjoyed at school, and now he had plenty of time for it. In the event she'd done better than that and brought him a set of watercolours, which delighted him. It was those, and the art programmes he started watching on TV, that kept him going.

At the end of the five months he discovered his final destination: Penzance. They'd driven him there in a single day – over four hundred miles. Then it was back to square one: another anonymous flat in a town he knew nothing about. Whatever confidence he'd built up in Norwich deserted him. He returned to his nocturnal lifestyle, frightened of every shadow.

And then, one evening, he turned on the TV and found a programme about the artist and mariner Alfred Wallis.

He was riveted. It wasn't just the magic of the paintings – the beautifully delineated old sailing ships, the subtle colours, the weird disregard for proportion and perspective; it was the extraordinary story of this man who'd gone to sea at the age of nine and sailed from Cornwall to Newfoundland. Not until the age of seventy had he turned to art, painting with enamel on whatever came to hand, from plates to odd-shaped pieces of cardboard; then he'd been taken up by some of the greatest British artists of the day – Ben Nicholson, Barbara Hepworth, Christopher Wood. Now his work was to be found in galleries across the world. One interviewee had travelled to Cornwall from Japan to study his work.

All this had happened under ten miles from where Kevin was sitting. Like him, Wallis had been lonely, painting 'for company' after his wife's death. It seemed like a sign. The next day, throwing caution to the winds, Kevin took a bus to St Ives.

Like so many before him, he fell instantly in love with the town. The fact that he was out in broad daylight for the first time in months, surrounded by crowds of people, only served to make the experience more dreamlike. He wondered at the harbour with its smartly painted fishing boats, wearing their protective buoys like party balloons; the tiny turnstones scurrying over the sun-bleached paving stones; the stacks of intricately woven lobster pots on Smeaton's Pier; the narrow, higgledy-piggledy old houses of Downalong; the dark, wave-lashed rocks edging the Island; the great expanse of Porthmeor Beach and the greater expanse of sea above it; and, at the heart of it all, a modest house – the one he was passing now – bearing a plaque to the memory of Alfred Wallis. He had not imagined that the sight of a simple building could touch him so deeply.

'I want to move to St Ives,' he told the witness protection officer next time they spoke.

She laughed. 'You and half of Britain. Have you any idea of property prices in that town? Anything halfway decent gets snapped up as a second home or holiday rental. Locals have hardly got a chance.'

Yet somehow she'd managed it: an old council flat, smaller and more basic than the two previous safe houses, but that didn't matter. Here Kevin felt that his new life was finally beginning, thanks to a long-dead mariner.

He raised his baseball cap to the plaque.

'Thanks, Alf,' he said.

### iii

'Out,' said Grigorski to the young woman lying beside him in the bed. 'Now.'

She groaned, but knew better than to protest. Gathering her clothes, she headed for the bathroom.

Grigorski examined himself in the wardrobe mirror. For a man in his mid-forties, he was in exceptionally good shape, his body – though it bore some spectacular scars – still firm and muscular. And there was no denying that his beard was a thing of splendour, much admired by the hipsters of Shoreditch.

Still, it was a strain, this double – or rather, triple – life. He couldn't afford to draw attention to himself at the gym, so he went at the quietest times and never bench-pressed as much as his stupendous maximum. To his neighbours and the girls he hooked up with he was Emil, a Romanian builder – a guise in which he could indulge to the full his appetite for vodka and sex. None of them could have guessed that when he left for work in the morning he carried with him the robes of an Orthodox priest, into which he changed at a different place each day en route to the cathedral in Knightsbridge.

'Couldn't I just be attached to the embassy?' he had pleaded with the General.

'Certainly not. The British keep files on every member of staff. They would have no difficulty in identifying you as one of ours.'

'A businessman, then?'

'With a flashy apartment and a BMW? No chance. The budget won't stretch to it.'

'But a priest… Suppose someone asks me about a weird point of theology?'

'Tell them it's a subject of particular interest to the Metropolitan, and they should ask him.'

'The Metropolitan?'

'The Archbishop. Surely you knew that? I think I'd better arrange a training course.'

So Grigorski had spent a month being schooled in the Orthodox faith by a defrocked priest who shuffled into his flat each morning as though carrying the full weight of his sins, and occasionally burst into tears at the thought of his disgrace.

'I suppose you'll do,' said the Metropolitan when Grigorski arrived in London. 'Just stay in the background until you've found your feet.'

The metaphor was all too apt. Services at the cathedral lasted for up to three hours. Grigorski had done plenty of sentry duty in his time, but it had never felt as demanding as standing in a cloud of incense while one of the real priests droned his way through the liturgy. Only a pair of expensive air-sole trainers made it bearable.

Today, however, he was spared divine office. He had an appointment with Oleg Ogorodnikov.

The oligarch's penthouse was a stone's throw from the cathedral, on a site previously occupied by a masterpiece of Brutalist architecture. When this building had been demolished, locals had breathed a sigh of relief, telling themselves that whatever replaced it could not conceivably be as bad. But they were wrong.

Jutting shamelessly above the surrounding cityscape, the block resembled a multi-storey car showroom. This was no coincidence, for the plans had originally been drawn up for just such an enterprise in Qatar. The architect, tipped off that his employers took years to settle their bills, had withdrawn from the deal and managed to foist his scheme on Ogorodnikov instead. Its most elegant feature was the lift, designed to ferry Lamborghinis up and down. It was in this that Grigorski now ascended.

His host was sitting in a black leather desk chair, surveying the city with the fierce intensity of a border guard in his watchtower.

'Good morning, Major,' he said. 'The girl in the nightclub – what have you got on her?'

'Anita Scott. Aged thirty-two. A journalist, according to her tax return; doesn't make much money from it. Wrote two articles about Durden Hall for a website you closed down, so that must have been her motivation. Voted for the Green Party in the last election, Labour in the two before that; no evidence of activism. Shares a flat in Streatham with her sister. Her medical records mention treatment for asthma. We've adjusted her credit rating so she won't get any loans if she asks for them. Do you want to leave it at that, or shall we rough her up a bit?'

'I think we can leave it at that. As the British say, we have bigger fish to fry. Let's see what Anton Ivanovich has to report about the diamond project.'

He activated the computer screen on his desk. The pallid face of a young man in his twenties took shape, fixing them with disconcertingly large eyes.

'Good morning, Lord Ogorodnikov.'

'Good morning, Anton Ivanovich. What is the route you suggest?'

The young man paused, then spoke as if reading from a script. 'For maximum profit with minimum exposure to money-laundering regulations, I suggest the following:

'1) Transfer blood diamonds from Angola to Nigeria in exchange for oil.

'2) Transfer oil by sea to Syria. Exchange for arms.

'3) Transfer arms to Afghanistan. Exchange for opium.

'4) Transfer opium to Pakistan and convert to heroin.

Exchange for uranium.

'5) Transfer uranium to Iran. Exchange for Abstract Expressionist works from the Mohammed Reza Shah collection.

'6) Transfer artworks to Monaco for sale to designated private collector.

'7) Transfer proceeds via Switzerland to the Cayman Islands.

'8) Transfer funds through your eight largest Cayman Islands companies. Use to purchase gilt-edged bonds on the London Stock Exchange.

'9) Liquidate bonds and transfer to Ogorodnikov Properties plc.

'These are the estimated profits at each stage.'

A bank of figures filled the screen. They started high and ended stratospheric.

'What's the risk rating, Anton Ivanovich?'

'Two per cent, as long as the protocols I have suggested are implemented.'

'And all of these steps meet the General's approved guidelines?'

'Confirmed. As you can see, his twenty per cent cut has been factored in. Disbursements to local operatives and officials account for a further one per cent.'

'I think we can live with that. Excellent work, Anton Ivanovich. Will you give the necessary instructions, and copy Major Grigorski in with extra encryption?'

'Of course, your lordship. Will that be all?'

'For now, yes.'

'He's a marvel, that Anton Ivanovich,' said Ogordnikov. 'I don't know how I ever did without him.'

'You wanted to discuss the other matter as well,' said Grigorski.

'Ah yes.' Ogorodnikov executed a 360-degree spin in his chair, a smile on his face. 'The other matter.'

### iv

After issuing exhaustive instructions to agents in ten countries, Anton decided he deserved some downtime.

He had been thinking about writing a novel. This was the time to start. Romance was, in his view, the most marketable genre.

But how to begin? So many words to choose from; so many possible ways of assembling them! Even to someone of his enormous capabilities, the prospect was daunting.

At last he hit on an opening sentence he felt sure would fit the bill.

'Most people agree,' he wrote, 'that an unmarried man with a lot of money needs a cohabitee.'

There!

# CHAPTER 5

## i

IN *CATHEDRAL*'S OFFICES, Pamela Pettifer was also struggling with the intractability of words. She could manage them well enough in academic papers, where any amount of leaden phrasing was permissible. But Alex Rosewater had insisted that something more fluent was required for the magazine.

'Do we really need a leader column?' she asked. 'Social media is where the action is.'

Rosewater agreed that #instinctivism was proving every bit the internet phenomenon he had hoped. 'But without the think pieces, those posts would be like – well, interplanetary craft without a mother ship. And this leader is going to be the most important thing you ever write.'

So, agonisingly, she ground it out.

'Our commitment to instinctivism is uncompromising, and we salute those who have identified foot-dragging in the sector for their courageous support of God's prior creations.

But without concrete policy actions, these investment principles will never be truly empowering. The time has come to call out elite spaces and hierarchies that have failed to engage with systemic change.

'For churches that truly respect instinctivism, the path is clear. God's prior creations must be made welcome at the altar rail to receive Holy Communion and tell their stories. Humans have no right to stand in their way.'

## ii

'I think you need to take this seriously, darling.'

'No, no.' The Archbishop of Canterbury put down his cup of tea, shaking his head wearily. Much as he valued his wife's advice, he was quite sure of his ground in this instance. 'I've seen this kind of thing before. These people have taken a step too far; whatever support they have gathered will just evaporate. To respond would simply lend them credibility.'

'Darling, I know you think that social media is the devil's work, and you may be right. But there's no telling what the *Cathedral* campaign could lead to. You must take a strong line – excommunicate Dr Pettifer if necessary.'

The Archbishop chuckled. 'Really, dear, you do get carried away sometimes. I hardly think excommunication will be necessary. Cut me another slice of carrot cake, would you?'

Walking for its own sake was not something Kevin had ever considered; but somehow the phrase 'coastal path', overheard one morning beside the lifeboat station, kept nagging at him. To think that you could walk along the edge of England for hundreds of miles with the great ocean gleaming beside you – the ocean that had so inspired Alfred Wallis!

A look at the map told him that the path could easily be picked up near Zennor. There was a bus service to the village, and from there it should only take him a couple of hours to walk back to St Ives.

He set off after lunch the next day. It was a sunny afternoon and he stopped for an ice-cream at the cheerful café in Zennor before making his way down through the fields to the coastal path itself.

The word 'path' made it sound easier-going than it was: rather than strolling nonchalantly along, he found himself scrambling over rocks for much of the way. But the views made it worthwhile: time and again he stopped to gaze spellbound at the dark, variegated cliffs sloping down to a sea that seemed to go on forever.

He met several groups of walkers coming the other way, all better kitted out than him, with proper hiking boots and rucksacks. But suddenly he realised that it was a long while since he'd seen anyone, and the light was beginning to fade, and St Ives was not yet in sight.

'Better get a move on,' he said to himself. And then he heard a noise.

It was a low groan, followed by a string of curses; then, more distinctly, 'Idiot, Ezra Cairns! Idiot! Idiot!'

Climbing over a large rock, Kevin saw the figure of an elderly man sprawled on the ground. He had a red face and long white hair and was clearly in pain. Beside him lay a yellow tweed cap and a rough stick. His eyes were full of relief as he gazed up at the new arrival.

'Hello, young man,' he said. 'This is no place to be walking in the middle of the night. You must be even stupider than I am.'

Kevin wondered whether the old man had suffered a blow to the head. 'It isn't the middle of the night,' he said. 'It's early evening.'

'You'll find that I'm given to exaggeration. But I'm not exaggerating the pain in my bloody ankle. I don't know whether I've sprained or broken it, but it hurts like hell. So don't just stand there – give me a hand up. We'll have to look lively if we're to make St Ives before dark.'

Ezra Cairns was a stout man and Kevin needed all his strength to set him on his feet. By the time they started along the path with the invalid's arm over his shoulder, he was already dripping with sweat. Cairns, for his part, proved a remarkably cheerful companion when not wincing with pain. From time to time he would break into improvised song:

> *If you don't want a swollen ankle in your sock,*
> *better keep away from the Cornish rocks!*
> *It's fun to start on the coastal path,*
> *but just watch out for the aftermath.*

'I was an adman in my youth,' he explained, 'and have never quite got over it, so the jingles just keep coming. Maybe I could make it as a rap artist. Or do you think my rhymes are too sophisticated?' He gave a deep chuckle.

The lights of St Ives were burning bright by the time the town came into view. The last stages of the path were smoother and free of rocks, though their narrowness presented a challenge.

'You'll be glad to hear that we're heading for Downalong,' said Cairns. 'I live over the shop. Not far now.'

Kevin had passed the little gallery a hundred times, and occasionally stared in at one of the exhibitions by local artists; but what lay at the back of it was a revelation. With its panoply of canvases and easels, its neatly arranged brushes and tubes of oil paint in every imaginable colour, Ezra Cairns' studio seemed to him an Aladdin's cave. To think that he himself had made do for all these months with a kitchen table and the most basic materials.

'Wow,' he said when he had settled Cairns on a chair. 'A place like this… I could be happy here for the rest of my life.'

Cairns laughed.

*Heaven it ain't,* he sang, *unless you're a paint-splattered saint.*

'But,' he said, 'I could do with some help here and in the gallery – packing, cleaning, that sort of thing; even a bit of social media, God help me. Would that be of any interest to you?'

Kevin couldn't believe his luck. 'Just one thing,' he said: 'Would you let me watch you paint?'

Ezra Cairns looked at him in astonishment. 'Why would

you want to do that?'

'Just to see how you do it. There's so much I need to learn, and you – you're a real artist.'

Cairns hesitated. 'I don't know. I don't have as much time as I'd like for my own work, and I need to concentrate. I'm not sure I want someone breathing down my neck.'

But Kevin could see that he was flattered. 'I'll be as quiet as the grave, swear to God. I just want to see how you do it. Even if it's only for an hour a week… It would make all the difference.'

Cairns looked around the studio as if hoping one of the canvases might offer some advice.

'All right,' he said at last. 'We'll give it a go.'


iv


It was just after eleven o'clock on a Tuesday night when Rupert Norris left the old guild hall and set off across London Bridge. Boozy dinners no longer played the part in his working life that they had done when he started out in banking, and his wife – mindful of his heart condition – insisted on a healthy regime at home. But tonight, instead of heading back to Hampshire, he was staying with his son James. This evening's gala had been a rare opportunity to enjoy most of a bottle of excellent Bordeaux, and he had not let it slip.

Not that he was drunk – or at least, only slightly. He was

sufficiently stout to absorb a good amount of alcohol. But his mood was certainly merry. As he reached the midpoint of his crossing, he broke into song:

*London Bridge is falling down, falling down, falling down,*
*London Bridge is falling down, my fair lady.*

He barely noticed the tall, well-built man coming towards him; he certainly failed to register the second one coming up behind. So he was taken completely unawares when the two bundled him over the parapet into the river below.

The cold water brought him back to sobriety in an instant. As he surfaced, gasping for breath, he registered the strength of the current, his distance from the lights on the bank, the absence of any craft that might come to his aid or an object that he might cling to. He has been a strong swimmer in his youth, but his waterlogged overcoat and his tightly laced shoes put him at an impossible disadvantage. The river bore him away, as it had so many others over the centuries, until his head disappeared below the surface for the last time and his struggles came to an end.

v

Ben was delighted to be commissioned by the *Sunday Times*. Perhaps his journalistic career was not at an end after all; perhaps a whole series of think pieces would follow. True, they had only asked him for eight hundred words, responding as the ex-editor of *Cathedral* to the magazine's call for animal Communion. But it was a start – and as his fingers skipped across the keyboard of his laptop, he gloried once more in the trade he had been born to.

'Little did I imagine,' he wrote, 'when I mused on the possibility of my dog possessing a soul, that I was opening Pandora's box. It was a perfectly reasonable proposition – but like so many reasonable propositions, it has been hijacked by fanatics peddling nonsensical ideas. I would like to believe that these have no chance of acceptance; history, however, suggests otherwise.

'That we should show compassion to all of creation goes without saying. But must we abandon common sense in order to pursue this goal? My answer is no.'

He read the article through with satisfaction. Working as a cocktail pianist at Chicane was enjoyable enough, but he knew it was not the best use of his talents. This would be a ringing fanfare, signalling his return to his vocation.

He clicked the 'Send' button.

vi

'You're looking cheerful,' said Hughie.

Ben told him the good news. 'And,' he said, glancing through the window, 'it's a beautiful day.'

'It is. In fact, I thought I might take the boat out. Why

don't you come along? God knows we could both do with some sunlight and fresh air. Much as I love my subterranean life, one has to surface occasionally.'

The boat was an antique launch moored at Westminster Pier.

'They don't generally allow civilian boats here,' said Hughie. 'Being so close to the Houses of Parliament, it's a high-security zone. But I have special dispensation.' He tapped the side of his nose. 'If you can make ready to cast off, I'll get the engine going.'

Ben was still grappling with the mooring ropes when a police patrol boat slowed and turned towards them.

'Nothing to worry about,' said Hughie. 'I've got to know most of the river police over the years. This looks like my friend Inspector Aziz.' He waved his arm. 'Morning, Aziz!'

'Morning, Captain Hughie!' The man at the wheel was slightly built and must have struggled to reach police height requirements, but exuded competence and cheerfulness. 'Any contraband on board?'

'In my dreams. Chicane must be supporting the Exchequer single-handed with the amount of tax we pay on booze. Any excitement on the river?'

'A bit of a fracas on one of the party boats last night, but that's par for the course. People, alcohol, confined space – it's a recipe for a punch-up, isn't it? Apart from that – a guy went over the side of London Bridge a couple of nights ago and hasn't been seen since. Let us know if you see anything.'

'We'll keep an eye out. Though to be honest, the last thing I want to come across today is a corpse.'

'I tell myself that every morning. But I'm not always that lucky. Take care, Hughie.'

Hughie and Ben set off downriver. Ben was not an instinctive sailor, but on a spring day like this, with the sun on his face and the ensign behind him flapping in a brisk breeze, he could fully understand the lure of open water. There was something strangely affecting about the synergy of the old boat, its woodwork varnished to the colour of molten toffee, and the great river hurrying to the sea. Whatever happened on its banks – whether men built artistically, as Christopher Wren had with his beautiful churches, or clumsily and for naked profit, like the developers of the ranks of 'prestige' flats – this was something that would never change. Mariners would always take the tide in search of adventure; the restless currents would always speed them on their way.

'"Anything wet and in the Met" – that's the river police motto,' said Hughie. 'It's not just the Thames that they're in charge of – it's the canals, the reservoirs, the little rivers. Anti-terrorism is a big part of it – making sure nobody blows up the bridges. Then there are the tow-path muggers, the flood victims, the paedophiles on narrow boats trying to lure kids on board. Old Aziz has his work cut out, one way or another.'

'He seems like a decent guy.'

'One of the best. And he has some good tales to tell. One of his first cases was the Millennium Dome raid, which you're probably too young to remember: half a dozen villains trying to steal three hundred and fifty million pounds' worth of diamonds. What they didn't know was that the police had rumbled them and were lying in wait. Aziz helped to collar the driver of the speedboat they planned to escape in.'

The bridges glided by – Waterloo, Blackfriars, Southwark, London, Tower. They had just passed St Katharine's Dock when a dark shape surfaced suddenly in the water ahead of them.

'Christ,' said Hughie. 'I hope that's not…'

But it was.

## vii

The minutes Ben spent pinning the body to the side of the launch with a boathook were among the longest of his life. He thanked God that Hughie had been able to reach Aziz at once on his mobile, and was there to keep the boat steady until the police arrived. Trying to pull the body from the water on their own was not something either of them fancied.

The journey down to the river police headquarters was a short one. A traditional blue lamp marked its pier. On the main pontoon stood a shallow steel basin with wheels, slightly discoloured by mud.

'In case you're wondering,' said Hughie, 'that primitive but useful piece of equipment is the Dead Body Reception Tray. It's basically a bath without a plug so that the water can drain away.'

Ben tried not to look at the bloated face of the new occu-pant. The dinner-jacket beneath the overcoat left little doubt as to his identity.

'Rupert Norris, sixty,' said Aziz. 'Worked in the City. Wife and two kids. Poor sod.'

'Suicide?' asked Hughie.

'That's a good question. According to the CCTV footage, he came out of the Embroiderers' Hall at 11.02 after a slap-up dinner, turned right, started to cross the bridge. A member of the public made an emergency call to report someone falling into the river at 11.06. So if he did jump, he didn't hang around – went pretty much straight in. And that's unusual. Most people spend a good while contemplating the awfulness of their existence before they take the plunge.'

'Maybe something happened at the dinner that made him completely desperate,' said Ben.

'It's possible. But the general impression is that he was enjoying himself, big time.'

'An accident, then?'

'That's more plausible. He may have decided to dance along the parapet. Drunks sometimes do – and by all accounts, he'd drunk a good deal of alcohol.'

'Or murder?' said Hughie. 'If so, it's unlikely to have resulted from an argument or a mugging gone wrong, given the narrow time frame. It would have had to be premeditated, with his movements being followed very carefully – perhaps by someone at the dinner.'

Aziz shrugged. 'As we like to say, we're keeping an open mind. And now I think we should get Mr Norris inside.'

Two large constables wheeled the body away. Ben and Hughie clambered back onto the launch. Hughie waved to Aziz as they turned upriver.

'The next time I promise to keep an eye out for something,' he said to Ben, 'don't let me.'

## viii

Anton Ivanovich was, unusually for him, having second thoughts. Examining the latest bestseller lists, he noted that historical fiction might be a better path to take than romance. But which period? The eighteenth century had definite possibilities.

At last it came to him: the French Revolution!

'It was an age that was unimprovable,' he wrote, 'but also an age that was incapable of deterioration.'

Much better!

# CHAPTER 6

### i

Four days later Ben took a morning train to Oxford. Opening the *Sunday Times*, he was gratified to find his article beside the main editorial, with a photograph of himself at the top. *Cathedral* had never carried photos of contributors, on the grounds that they encouraged a sense of self-importance. He now rather regretted the rule.

It was a short walk from Oxford Station to Ben's house, across Hythe Bridge and up Walton Street. As he approached it, he was surprised to see a small but noisy crowd spilling from the pavement onto the road.

His first thought was that they must be partying students, about to head for one of the restaurants on Little Clarendon Street or a picnic on Port Meadow. Then again, they could have come from church: he remembered that there was a big-name preacher in town. But as he drew closer, the scene took on a more sinister aspect.

A bearded figure with a spray can was putting the final touches to an inscription under Ben's front window. 'PETPHOBIC SCUM!' it read. 'INSTINCTIVISM NOW!'

The message appeared to resonate with the crowd.

'Scum!' they chanted. 'Scum! Scum! Scum!'

Several of them, Ben noticed, were wearing T-shirts with the All God's Creatures logo. The nearest was a young woman carrying a copy of the *Sunday Times*.

She glanced towards him, and their eyes locked. He prayed that she hadn't seen his photo by-line – but in vain.

'It's him!' she shouted.

A score of faces turned towards him. The look on them recalled all too vividly the oligarch's bodyguard at Chicane as boeuf Stroganoff dripped down his shirtfront. Clearly, they were in no mood to parley.

'Get him!' someone yelled.

Ben turned and ran.

He had been a good middle-distance runner at school, and could still outpace most men of his age. But his fitness had declined as Molly grew infirm and their exhilarating runs together gave way to gentle rambling along the towpath. Jogging in St James's Park before the evening's work at Chicane had gone only a little way to getting him back in shape.

Desperation, however, gave him an edge. Before the crowd could react, he had bolted down the street and reached its junction with the Woodstock Road.

To his left lay the comparatively open spaces of North Oxford; to his right, the city centre, with a greater concentration of people and a more intricate arrangement of streets and alleyways. His instinct told him to turn right.

The first stretch of pavement was empty enough; he hurtled past a young mother with a pram and a man weighed down with carrier bags. If only he could reach Carfax, the main shopping street, his chances of escaping down the byways leading off it were good.

But he had reckoned without a crowd of foreign-language students in yellow baseball caps emerging suddenly from around a corner thirty yards ahead of him. He had no choice but to cross the road – and with streams of traffic coming from both directions, that was easier said than done.

'Stop him!' The mob, headed by a young man built like a university rugby player, was gaining on him. 'Stop the bastard!'

Ben took the plunge, dodging between a tour bus and the car behind it, drawing a long blast from the car's horn. He was halfway across. But the southbound traffic was moving faster, offering fewer opportunities.

A small gap in front of another bus seemed his best bet. With all the speed that was left in him, he dashed in front of it. But as he did so, he stumbled. Instead of following a straight line across its path, he staggered towards it.

The bus braked and swerved, missing him by inches. As he struggled to regain his balance, he collided with a student on a bicycle, toppling with him onto the pavement. He registered a sharp pain in his right ankle.

'Sorry,' he said as he disentangled himself. 'So sorry.'

But there was no time to stop. Ahead of him was the entrance to St John's College. He plunged through it and saw to his relief that the barrier deterring tourists was open.

His ankle was hurting badly now – so badly that he knew he couldn't run much further. Unless he found a hiding place fast, he would be cornered by the mob.

He turned left in the first quadrangle and hobbled towards the nearest archway. It opened onto a well-worn stone staircase. He forced himself up it.

A door on the first landing was slightly ajar. He pushed it open to find a dark-haired woman standing in the middle of a book-lined room.

'Please,' he gasped. 'They're after me.'

The woman smiled. 'Well, well,' she said. 'If it isn't Sir Lancelot.'

For a moment, Ben was baffled. Then it dawned on him. The woman was the Stroganoff-throwing diner from Chicane.

'Who's after you?' she asked. 'The Russians?'

He shook his head. 'Fanatics.'

'Through there.' She pointed to a door on the other side of the room. 'I'll deal with them.'

The door led into a dark, musty bedroom. Discarded clothes were piled on every surface. Ben lay down on the floor behind the bed, his heart still racing.

Almost at once there was a pounding of feet on the stairs below. Then there were voices, too close for comfort: close enough to have entered the next room.

The words that followed were too muffled to make out, but their tone was easy to gauge: a burst of aggression from the intruders; an indignant response from the dark-haired woman; a general muttering of the mob. Then, incredibly, a clattering retreat down the stairs. The confrontation was over almost as soon as it had begun.

Ben rose from behind the bed and slowly opened the door. His saviour was buttoning her shirt.

'A piece of advice my aunt once gave me,' she said. 'If you want to bring unruly people to their senses, take off some of your clothes. If the shock doesn't do it, the embarrassment will. Does that make us quits?'

'I think it does.'

'I told them I'd seen you through the window climbing down a drainpipe. I don't think they'll be back.'

'Thanks.' He sat down wearily on a chair, massaging his ankle.

'So what was all that about?'

He told her.

'You were playing with fire,' she said, 'writing an article like that.'

'It was a plea for moderation.'

'Those people don't know the meaning of the word.'

'I wonder if any of them are still hanging around my house.'

'I could go over and check for you. I need to get something for lunch anyway. Jane never has anything in the fridge.'

'Jane?'

'My cousin. These are her rooms. I had a party to go to in Summertown last night, and she was away for the weekend, so she said I could doss down here. I thought I'd give it a bit of a tidy as a thank you – but as you can see, I haven't got very far. Have you eaten?'

'Not yet.'

'So where's your house?'

'If you go to the far end of Pusey Street you'll see it just across the road. You'll recognise it by the graffiti, or the baying mob if they're still there.'

'I'll see what I can find. I'm Anita, by the way.'

'I'm Ben.'

'See you in a bit.'

Ben took out his phone and checked his emails. One was from the *Sunday Times*. His article had prompted an enormous online response: would he care to write a follow-up for next weekend?

At least some people could see sense, he thought. But when he examined the newspaper's website, he found that the enormous response was almost entirely negative.

'Who does Ben Fairweather think he is?' demanded one reader. 'And why is your newspaper giving oxygen to his abhorrent, outdated ideas? Unless the *Sunday Times* signs up to the Instinctivism Pledge, I shall report you to the Hate Speech and Macro-Triggering Board.'

Others were more blunt.

'Fairweather is a filthy bigot who should check his privilege. Stop privileging his despicable views. May he rot in hell.'

Ben thought that perhaps he wouldn't write a follow-up article.

Anita returned with a take-away.

'Indian all right with you?'

'Fine. As long as it isn't too spicy.'

'There might be the odd chilli. No point in a vindaloo

without chilli.'

'But equally, no point in setting your mouth on fire so you can't actually taste anything.'

'There we'll have to differ. Anyway, I stopped by your gaff and there was a policeman outside. Apparently someone turned up with a Molotov cocktail. He was persuaded not to throw it, but they think you should lie low for a while. There's a number for you to call.'

Ben rang it.

'I'm afraid you've made yourself very unpopular, sir,' said the voice at the other end. 'We recommend that you absent yourself from the property for the next few weeks. Have you got somewhere else you can stay?'

'Yes, but it's not ideal.'

'Better safe than sorry. In this case, judging from the activity on social media, much better. Goodbye, sir.'

Ben reached for a poppadom and chewed it cautiously.

'I can give you a lift back to London if you like,' said Anita.

'That would be great. I think I'll avoid public transport for a bit.'

'It's just an old banger of a van, I'm afraid. Handy for architectural salvage, but not exactly luxurious.'

The vindaloo was everything Ben feared it might be.

'This passion for architecture – where does it come from?' he asked when he finally regained the power of speech.

'My father, indirectly. He was a brass-rubbing enthusiast, and he used to take me to churches with him. There was something magical about seeing these figures take shape on the paper – like watching a ghost materialise. What I really loved, though, was the buildings – the look of them, the smell of them, the whole atmosphere. This was long before the Great Awakening, of course, so they weren't much used. But their elegance and their sense of history just bowled me over.

'So all my teens were spent looking forward to training as an architect. And what happened when I got to college? Did they tell us how to design a flying buttress or a hyperbolic paraboloid roof? Did they hell. It was straight into planning law. And I just thought, 'I can't be doing with this.' So I started writing about architecture instead, and found I was quite good at it. The irony is that, with so many threats to old buildings, I'm now rather an expert on planning law.'

'And Lord Ogorodnikov – do you think he's up to more dodgy business?'

'Oh yes. 'Anita took a bite of samosa. 'Lord Ogorodnikov is as dodgy as they come.'

## ii

Anita's van was a boneshaker by any standards. It rattled alarmingly; what remained of the seats' padding was barely held in place by industrial quantities of tape.

'I hope you don't mind a small detour to pick up a door,' she said.

'A door?'

'You'll see.'

They stopped at a church on the outskirts of the city. A skip had been placed outside it, and part of the west wall fenced off; notices warned of the need for safety clothing. A banner proclaimed 'Considerate Constructors'. Someone had added the letters I and N to the first word.

'There it is,' said Anita. 'On top of the skip. Give us a hand, would you?'

It was a small but beautiful door, its fine oak timbers punctuated with rusty iron studs. Ben wondered how many people, long dead, had turned the key in the great lock.

'It's amazing,' he said. 'Why are they chucking it out?'

'You of all people should know that.' Anita ran her fingers reverently over the ancient wood. 'The parochial church council decided that it was too narrow for worshippers bringing larger animals to Communion, so it had to go. They've knocked a hole in the wall which is twice the size.'

'Don't they need permission to do that?'

'Officially, yes. But there's a no-holds-barred battle going on among the Church Commissioners which means they're struggling to enforce the rules. There are acts of vandalism like this happening all over the country. England hasn't seen anything like it since the Puritan iconoclasts in the seventeenth century.'

Ben shook his head. It was not just that he shared Anita's dismay; it was the fact that this had been happening without his knowledge. As editor of *Cathedral*, he would have had his finger on the pulse and led a campaign against it. Now he was just a nightclub pianist, playing lounge music while the country descended into bitter factionalism.

'Oh God,' he prayed as he and Anita slid the disenfranchised door into the back of the van, 'help me turn the tide of this madness.'

### iii

Kevin sipped at his glass of beer. It was getting close to closing time and only a handful of drinkers were left on the benches outside the small harbour pub. In front of them the vague silhouettes of the fishing fleet rode at anchor, while across the dark expanse of water the lights of Carbis Bay and Hayle gleamed companionably. And the quietness! Only the lapping of the sea and the voices of the other drinkers... To them it was just another evening, but to Kevin it all seemed magical. This was something he felt he had never known before. This was peace.

And above all, there was the girl sitting opposite him. He and Donna could hardly have met in a more farcical way: he being rash enough to open a bag of chips on the harbour wall, she shouting a warning – just too late – as one of the town's ruthlessly predatory seagulls swooped down to snatch it from his hand. But they'd got talking, and she'd mentioned her job as an assistant curator at Lyle St Ives, and he'd been full of questions about the collection...and here they were.

'So how's Squire Trelawny?' she asked.

Kevin looked baffled. 'Who?'

'The guy you work for.'

'His name's not Trelawny – it's Ezra Cairns. And he's not a squire. At least, I don't think he is. What do you have to do to be a squire?'

Donna laughed. 'It's just my name for him. Squire Trelawny is the name of a character in *Treasure Island*. Haven't you read it?'

'No.' The truth was that Kevin hadn't read many books – but he didn't want this bright girl with the most beautiful eyes to know that.

'You should – it's absolutely brilliant. Anyway, Trelawny is a classic Cornish name, and I just think Ezra Cairns looks like a good old-fashioned squire presiding benevolently over his feasting tenants. That broad face, broad forehead, flat nose, flowing white hair – perfect!'

'He doesn't come from Cornwall. He's lived in St Ives for thirty years, but he's really from Kent.'

Donna laughed again. 'How many of the people you meet do come from Cornwall? Not you, not me, hardly any of my colleagues at the Lyle: most of us are Londoners.'

'Ezra calls me the sorcerer's apprentice,' Kevin continued. 'There's so much I've learnt from him, I can't tell you. Yes, it was just an hour a week to start with, but it soon became more than that; and as for me keeping shtum, forget it: turned out he liked having a good natter while he was painting. The man's a born teacher – he just hadn't realised it. So I've lucked out, big time.'

'It wasn't luck,' said Donna. 'It was karma.'

'What's karma?'

'It's a popular chicken dish served in Indian restaurants.

No, seriously, it's the idea that what goes around comes around. You helped Ezra out of the kindness of your heart, and him teaching you to paint has been your reward.'

'I don't know about that. It just feels like everything's luck.'

'Apart from the war between your boss and my boss.'

Kevin laughed. 'Apart from that.'

'Which kind of makes us like Romeo and Juliet.' She raised her glass. 'To star-crossed lovers!'

Kevin wasn't quite sure what she was on about. But there was no doubt that the world 'lovers' sounded very promising.

He clinked his glass against hers.

<br>

**iv**

<br>

'I think I would like to buy Kensington Palace,' said Oleg Ogorodnikov. 'It has an excellent location and great development potential.'

The Prime Minister laughed nervously.

'I'm afraid it's not for sale, Oleg.'

'Not for sale? I thought this was a capitalist nation. In my own country, despite its legacy of Communism, everything is for sale.'

'We believe in the free market, of course. But some things are sacrosanct – including, I'm afraid, royal residences.'

'You sold Admiralty Arch. You sold the BBC Television Centre. Why not Kensington Palace?'

'Might you consider Chequers instead, Oleg? There could

be some flexibility there.'

The two men were fishing on Ogorodnikov's Berkshire estate. Not that there was much sport involved: the lake was so well stocked that it was almost impossible to cast without a fat trout taking the bait.

'To tell you the truth,' said Ogorodnikov, 'this country is beginning to irritate me. There is so much I could do here with my money, but so little that is not governed by tiresome regulations. Even if I put a billion dollars in gold under your nose, you would find a way to stop me spending it.'

'We're doing what we can to ease all these money-laundering checks, Oleg. No one in the City likes them. But we must be seen to go through the motions.'

'The only motions I care about are when I go to the toilet.'

A phone rang.

'It's Anton Ivanovich, your lordship,' said his PA.

Ogorodnikov grunted. Handing his fishing rod to a game-keeper, he took the phone and walked over to a boathouse modelled on Snow White's cottage.

'Where have we got to, Anton Ivanovich?'

'The artworks have arrived in Monaco. The purchaser is ready to take collection. However, from my projections for the exchange rate over the next week, you could realise an extra two million dollars by postponing the sale until next Thursday. Would you like me to action that?'

'Are the pictures safe in the meantime?'

'All necessary precautions have been taken.'

'Very well.'

Ogorodnikov stared at the likenesses of the Seven Dwarfs

carved into the eaves of the boathouse. Bashful and Sneezy seemed to him particularly well executed.

Anton Ivanovich was the best in the business, no doubt about it. But how ridiculous that you had to jump through so many hoops just to turn blood diamonds into prime London property. Yes, something certainly had to be done – and he was now quite clear that the Prime Minister could not be relied upon to do it.

v

The Prime Minister still smelt vaguely of fish when he arrived back at 10 Downing Street. He sent the six trout he had brought with him to the kitchens, requesting that the menu for dinner be altered. His catch would be something to impress the American ambassador with.

'Lightly grilled with a touch of fennel,' he instructed. 'And the best Chablis.'

Two of his special advisers were waiting for him. Natalie, a severe-looking young woman in a sharp suit, spoke first.

'You need a dog, Prime Minister.'

'A dog?' There was a sarcastic edge to his voice. Natalie was a smart cookie, but some of her ideas were rather too left-field. 'Why not a cat? Or a pushme-pullyou, come to that?'

'I'm not joking. All God's Creatures is the biggest rogue movement this country has seen since the Brexit Party. You need to establish your instinctivist credentials. We have reliable reports that the leader of the Opposition is about to purchase a sheep.'

'Then at least she'll have one loyal follower.'

'Unless we move fast, *you* will be seen as following her lead. I have a contact at the Kennel Club ready to action this. All we have to do is decide on the breed.'

The Prime Minister sighed. 'Very well. But you're in charge of walking it. What about a Labrador?' His uncle had had a chocolate Labrador. Playing with Labby on Holkham Beach was a vivid childhood memory.

'Too middle-class. You need something with wider appeal.'

'A Staffy? That would be good for the drug-dealer vote.'

'Please take this seriously, Prime Minister. The dog must be one that can travel with you and attend public events without causing anxiety.'

'French bulldogs are very popular,' said Duncan, the junior adviser.

The Prime Minister glared. 'Don't be ridiculous. Incredibly ugly and incredibly unpatriotic.'

'A Jack Russell, then.'

The Prime Minister drummed his fingers on the desk. Yes, he could see himself with a Jack Russell: a spirited, character-ful little dog symbolic of the best of Britain. It could nestle beside him on the front bench during PMQs; perhaps even be trained to growl at the leader of the Opposition, startling her sheep.

'Do it,' he said.

The 'war' between Ezra Cairns and Donna's boss was ostensibly about a parking space. This, however, was merely the touchpaper for a keg of gunpowder long waiting to explode.

In a town of narrow thoroughfares, parking spaces were as rare as spring picnickers. Few houses had their own; empty slots in the car parks within easy reach of the seafront appeared once in a blue moon.

Local people found their own solutions to this problem. Workmen brazenly parked their vans nose-to-tail in the least-used backstreets; the few residents lucky enough to have parking spaces they didn't need rented them out for handsome cash payments. It was in one of these that Ezra Cairns had berthed his Renault 4 van for several years.

Then, to his deep dismay, the owner asked for the space back.

'I've got my uncle coming for a long stay,' she said. 'He's not very mobile, so he'll need the car close by.'

Ezra imagined a Reliant Robin adapted for a paraplegic. But the vehicle that materialised was very different: an enormous white Range Rover. And it did not take long to discover that the owner was not Ruth Pascoe's uncle, but Quentin Eldridge-Cattermole, the director of Lyle St Ives.

'I'm sorry, Mr Cairns,' she said, 'but he offered me twenty pounds a week more than you. And with the cost of living…'

'You lied to me.'

'I'm sorry, Mr Cairns, but it was part of the deal. He didn't want anyone to know.'

In that case, thought Ezra, he's even stupider than I thought.

'The worst of it is that he's *already* got a parking space,' he fumed to Kevin. 'The Lyle provides one which he uses for his electric runaround. But is he content with that? No! He has to have another for that vulgar white monstrosity so that he can show off to his posh London friends when they come to stay. Greedy bastard!'

Kevin said nothing, thinking that he too would like to have a Range Rover in need of a parking space. But further conversations with Ezra suggested that his hostility towards Quentin Eldridge-Cattermole was more to do with art than with motor cars.

'I've sat at the same dinner table as him,' said Ezra, 'and I've never met anyone so pleased with himself. Bloody curators! They're the biggest parasites on the planet.'

'What do curators do, exactly?'

'It mainly involves sucking up to important people, ideally over an expensive lunch, and then basking in their reflected glory. You also have to practise being as pretentious as possible and talking in a language no one else understands. You should hear Eldridge-Cattermole pontificating on some of the ridiculous stuff he's given exhibition space to.

'I admit that not everything I sell in this gallery is a work of genius. It's like a bookshop: you've got to sell Agatha Christie as well as Proust if you're going to make ends meet. Most people who come here want straightforward decorative harbour views, so I sell them alongside the more interesting stuff. I wouldn't put them on my own walls, but they're well executed and fairly priced, and I'm not pretending they're more important than they are.

'I bet you anything you like that right now that Eldridge-Cattermole is running around like a headless chicken trying to drum up anything that might be called instinctivist. Because although people in the museum world fawn on him, he's fundamentally a philistine, and he's guilty of the biggest sin of all: imagining that politicians are more important than artists.'

Kevin respected Ezra's opinion on most things, but surely, he thought, Quentin Eldridge-Cattermole couldn't be *that* bad. Donna would hardly be working for him if he was.

His chance to find out was to come soon enough.

## vii

After two false starts, Anton Ivanovich was confident that he had cracked it. His book was to be an enigmatic, highly atmospheric *Bildungsroman* set in nineteenth-century England. He already had a title for it: *A Lot To Look Forward To*.

He set to work on Chapter One.

'I'm called Pip,' he wrote. 'I've got a brother-in-law called Joe Gargery.'

Very promising!

# CHAPTER 7

### i

'I'M GOING TO GO MAD,' said Ben. 'It's very kind of Hughie to let me use the flat, and it was fine as long as I could go home to Oxford at weekends. But being cooped up here until the police say it's safe to go back – I just don't think I can take it.'

Svetlana looked up from her spreadsheet. It was that strange twilight time when Chicane was set up for the evening but the first members were unlikely to show for another hour.

'Don't you have a friend you could stay with?'

Ben shook his head. 'All the London ones are married with children. I wouldn't want to impose, even if I didn't have such odd working hours.'

'So you need a place with a bit of room, not too far from the club, sharing with someone who won't disturb you during the day and doesn't mind you coming back in the early hours?'

'Exactly.'

'Then I've got an idea. You don't have to say yes, but…'

Was she about to suggest that he share with her? Ben's mind reeled at the prospect: swapping his sparse bachelor quarters for a femme fatale's den littered with high-end shopping bags, designer shoes and silk stockings – if women still wore silk stockings…

'The thing is,' said Svetlana, 'my granny could do with a bit of company. She's got this big old flat in South Kensington and she rattles around in it. She's very independent for an 85-year-old, and she's still got her marbles. She wouldn't admit for a moment that she was lonely, but I know that, underneath it all, she is. I think it would give her a real boost to have you living there, even if it was only for a few weeks. She wouldn't ask much in the way of rent, but maybe you could help out with shopping or a bit of DIY. And you needn't worry about disturbing her when you come back from this place, because she can't hear a thing once she's taken her hearing aid out. Think about it.'

## ii

Mrs Petrovna's flat was of a type familiar to Ben: well located and generously proportioned, but unimproved since the 1970s and in need of more than one coat of paint. The ancient boiler provided a continuous soundscape, clearing its throat before firing up like a rocket preparing to launch; the radiators clanked. Spiders, taking advantage of the occupant's short sight, had colonised the upper reaches of the kitchen and bathroom.

Ben's grandparents had had a flat like this; so had a couple of *Cathedral* contributors who had become family friends. When they died, new owners stripped every room, knocked down walls and imposed a decorative scheme that would itself seem hopelessly old-fashioned before long. It was, he mused, an apt metaphor for politically correct thought.

But if the flat was down-at-heel, it was also remarkably cosy. Heavy curtains in deep colours flanked the windows; rugs of exotic design sprawled across the drawing-room floor; chintz cushions were piled high on the sofa. On the walls were bright, dynamic designs for stage sets and costumes from the Ballets Russes, while dimly mysterious icons stared down from the top of a bookcase. On the shelves below them huddled sets of richly bound volumes, their spines busy with Cyrillic lettering.

It seemed certain to Ben that Mrs Petrovna must possess the thick Slavic accent that her daughter lacked. But again he was disappointed.

'Welcome, welcome!' she said in a voice suggestive of pre-war Home Counties tennis parties. 'Svetlana, darling, would you put the kettle on? There are some biscuits in the tin.'

She was a tiny woman whose shrewd gaze seemed to weigh Ben up in a moment. She wore an elegant silk blouse with pearls and a well-cut tweed skirt; her white hair was pinned in an impeccable bun.

'Do sit down,' she said, directing Ben to an armchair.

'Svetlana tells me you're a pianist.'

'At the moment, yes.'

Ben gave a brief account of his metamorphosis from magazine editor to nightclub entertainer.

'How very trying for you,' said Mrs Petrovna. 'And now you're a wanted man.'

'You could say that.'

'As you can see, I have plenty of room here. My family are always trying to persuade me to downsize, as they call it – but this place holds so many memories. And, of course, it's very handy for the cathedral.'

'Granny goes to the Russian Orthodox Cathedral in Knightsbridge,' Svetlana explained.

'There is a sense of exile to which the Orthodox Church speaks,' said Mrs Petrovna. 'The icons you see up there' – she pointed to the bookcase – 'have been in the family for generations. When my parents fled Russia in the Civil War, they carried them with them in their suitcases.'

'You never thought of moving back there?'

'No. This is where I was brought up; this is where my friends and family are. Svetlana feels a much stronger attachment to the old country than I do, don't you, darling?'

'I suppose so, Granny.'

'You'll want to see the spare room before you make a decision, Ben. Svetlana will show you where it is.'

The room with its single bed felt sparse after the rich furnishings of the drawing room. But it had a big window and a view over the street which seemed like a godsend after the dingy courtyard glimpsed from the flat above Chicane. Ben said he would take it.

'I'll bring my things over tomorrow, if that's all right.'

'Whatever suits you, dear,' said Mrs Petrovna.

As he left, Ben's eye fell upon a glass case in the corner of the drawing room. It was hinged and velvet-lined, and it contained a revolver.

'My late husband's,' said Mrs Petrovna. 'He was an excellent shot – won lots of competitions with it. I should probably have handed it into the police, but I couldn't bring myself to part with it. Is that ridiculously sentimental of me?'

'Of course not, Granny,' said Svetlana.

'See you tomorrow,' said Ben.

'See you tomorrow, dear.'


### iii


Oleg Ogorodnikov's phone rang. Not one of the phones his assistants answered on his behalf, but *his* phone. Its number was only known to four people – including the man he feared most. And, indeed, it was the Chairman of the Party calling now.

'Greetings, Oleg.'

'Greetings, sir.'

'Or should I say *Lord Ogorodnikov*? They tell me you have been elevated to the peerage. I should be grateful that you deign to talk to a commoner like me.'

Ogorodnikov blenched. What on earth was the Chairman

playing at?

'But sir,' he stammered. 'You approved it. I said to you, "Is it all right if I buy a British title?"'

'I can recall no such conversation. Are you suggesting that my mind is failing?'

'No, sir, nothing could be further—'

'I have always taken pride in our great tradition of egalitarianism.'

It's a stitch-up, thought Ogorodnikov. Horrifying vistas opened in front of him: his Russian assets confiscated; a hit squad dispatched. Perhaps Grigorski had already received orders, was even now stirring poison into his tea. How could he have been so naïve? He was used to dealing with ruffians – his entire friendship circle merited the term – but the Chairman was in another league.

There might still be a chance. If he could only get to his private jet…

'So, your lordship…'

'Yes, sir?'

There was silence at the end of the line – and then, suddenly, a burst of laughter.

'Got you, Oleg! Had you worried there, didn't I?'

'Well, yes…'

'Just my joke! Just my little jokey-wokey! Ha ha ha ha!'

'Ha ha,' said Ogorodnikov weakly. He sank back into his chair.

'Now listen, my friend. I need you to put some extra money through your system. You OK with that?'

'How much are we talking about, sir?'

'Another ten billion.'

The feeling of relief went as quickly as it had come.

'We're not really geared to that amount of money yet,' he said. 'Perhaps in a year…'

'I'm talking about weeks, Oleg. This has to be done before the new sanctions come into force. Don't disappoint me.'

The phone went dead. Ogorodnikov gazed out at the London skyline which once held so much promise. He had been set an almost impossible task, and his life depended on accomplishing it.

He rang Grigorski and Anton Ivanovich.

'We need to accelerate the programme,' he said.

## iv

Donna had never seen Quentin Eldridge-Cattermole so tetchy.

'Really, it's too much,' he said, staring at his computer. 'Here I am, trying to improve the gallery's instinctivist credentials, and what support do I get from London? None – or virtually none. Look what they've offered me from the stores, the wretches!'

Donna leaned over his shoulder to study the six images on his screen. Four of them, the quintessence of Victorian kitsch, showed wide-eyed kittens in bonnets and crinolines shopping, dining, dancing and attending the opera. The fifth, entitled *Waiting For His Master*, showed a spaniel staring wistfully from a window. Finally, there was a Cubist study of a bear – though, being Cubist, it could equally have been a sheep or a large rodent.

'Surely the kittens can find a place somewhere,' said Donna. 'We can present the series as a critique of the nineteenth-century bourgeoisie. And Barbara Hepworth was a cat-lover, wasn't she? There's an obvious connection with her oak-and-string sculptures – that cat's-cradle vibe.'

Eldridge-Cattermole grunted.

'And the other two would be good for the shop,' Donna continued. 'I can see a gorgeous spaniel tote bag, and the Cubist bear could make a great jigsaw.'

Eldridge-Cattermole grunted again. 'They're good ideas, but it's a drop in the ocean. And don't forget that we've got that party of journalists coming down: how am I going to explain all these spaces with barely any of God's prior creations in sight? We'll be written off as human-centric, and I'll be the one who carries the can.'

'What about the seagull project? Ines can't wait to get going on that. All we need is some fish and chips as bait.'

Ines, the senior curator, had made an eloquent presentation for the project some weeks before. It involved enticing as many seagulls as possible into one of the main exhibition spaces and keeping them there, well fed, for several days. By the time they were released, they would have covered the floor with their droppings, lending it a fascinating texture.

'Like Jackson Pollock,' said Ines.

Everyone was impressed, apart from the head of cleaning services, whose job it would eventually be to remove the installation. 'More bollocks than Pollock, I reckon,' he said.

In the event, he need not have worried.

'I've just heard back from the health and safety people,' Eldridge-Cattermole told Donna. 'They said however we went about it, it would be a Class A hazard. So that's that.'

'Well, then…'

Donna racked her brains. What on earth could be done to save the situation?

Suddenly she had an idea.

'The thing is,' she said, 'there's a young local artist I know called Kevin Jackson. He's a great admirer of Alfred Wallis, and he's done some really brilliant copies of his work. He's taught himself to paint on cardboard in the same way – he absolutely loves the technical side – and you, or at least I, couldn't tell them from the real thing.

'Now, God's prior creations barely feature in any of Wallis's paintings, beyond the odd fish or seagull – but supposing they did throughout? How would it alter his legacy? We could have an exhibition asking that question. We get Kevin to redo his copies with a dog here and a cat there, and we're away.'

Eldridge-Cattermole's eyes brightened. 'It could just work,' he said, 'if he's as good as you say. I can see the poster now: '*Ship's Cats and Sea Dogs – Redeeming Alfred Wallis.* Lyle St Ives introduces an important new instinctivist artist.' Well done, Donna! Tell your friend I'd like to meet him as soon as possible.'

'I don't know,' said Kevin. 'If Alfred Wallis had wanted ship's cats in his pictures, he'd have painted some, wouldn't he?'

'He might well have if he'd lived in a more right-thinking age,' said Donna, 'though of course we can't be sure. But the point is that we don't want him written out of history. This exhibition would be a way of saying, OK, he was misguided, but his work is still important.'

'I don't know. To be honest, I feel I've gone as far as I can with Alf. I've learnt a lot from him, but now I'm getting more from copying other painters: I've done a Ben Nicholson and I'm just starting a Matisse. I'd love to show them to you.'

'And I'd love to see them. But will you do this first – for me? It would earn me lots of brownie points with Quentin.'

Kevin sighed. 'All right, then… For you.'

'Thank you.' She kissed him.

'And more importantly, it'll be brilliant for you too,' she continued. 'It'll get your name out there as a young artist to watch. I'll see that the press office arranges some interviews; we might even get some local TV.'

Kevin looked alarmed. 'No, no,' he said. 'I wouldn't want any of that.'

'Why not?'

'Because…' Kevin thought quickly. 'Because I wouldn't want Ezra to know about it. He'd go spare if he thought I was getting chummy with your boss. And I owe him so much.'

'I suppose you could be anonymous: that always intrigues

people. Or a mystery collective.'

'What's a collective?'

'A group who work together, usually with a weird name. We'd have to think of one – ideally something good and Cornish.'

'Like what?'

'Like…Trelawny. It could be a secret homage to Ezra Cairns.'

'Sounds a bit boring to me.'

'OK. How about Brawny Trelawny? Or Scrawny Trelawny?'

Kevin nodded. 'I like that: got a bit of edge to it. Scrawny Trelawny.'

'Then that's settled.'


## vi

The Very Reverend Cecil Simpson was enjoying a new lease of life. It was two years since he had taken retirement – a state which did not sit easily with him. His career in the Church had been long and varied: he had managed a mission in Malawi, and another deep in the Peruvian jungle; he had ministered to drug addicts and battered wives in Glasgow; he had run silent retreats on a tidal island in the Hebrides, and held high office in two of England's finest cathedrals. He was a man used to challenges – and doing crosswords, however cryptic, in a London home for superannuated clergy did not come close to his definition of the word. True, the voluntary positions on two ecclesiastical bodies provided a degree of stimulation, but more often than not they involved sitting through tediously bureaucratic discussions. In short, he had champed at the bit.

So an invitation to stand in for an old friend as vicar of a Hertfordshire parish had fallen like the blessed dew from heaven. The friend, with a characteristic dislike of doing things by halves, had undergone operations on both his hips which left him immobilised. The benefice team was already short-staffed as a result of a widely publicised affair between the safeguarding officer and the musical director. The young seminarian initially sent to fill the breach had arrived with a pet mouse and spoken of All God's Creatures with a wild-eyed zeal which alarmed the older man. Instead, he called upon Cecil Simpson.

The benefice was a welcoming one. Cecil's temporary parishioners were keen on baking, and plied him with Victoria sponges, fairy cakes and cheese scones. If the turn-out for Holy Communion was relatively small – between a hundred and two hundred souls – it was still a good deal higher than anything he had been used to before the Great Awakening.

As a result of the musical director's suspension, he found choir practice added to his duties; but being possessed of a pleasant baritone voice, he considered this a treat rather than an imposition. He was just locking up after the Tuesday night practice, a *Nunc Dimittis* still on his lips, when a burly man with a dark beard appeared in the transept.

'Can I help you?' Cecil enquired.

The man smiled. 'Reverend Simpson! Surely you remember

me? We met at that fascinating lecture about Mount Athos. Father Peter from the Orthodox Cathedral.'

'Ah, yes,' said Cecil uncertainly, remembering the lecture but not Father Peter. 'How are things there?'

'Good, thank you, very good, God be praised. You mentioned that you were helping out here, and I happened to be passing by, and saw the lights on. So I said to myself, 'Why not stop by and say hello?''

If it seemed strange that a Russian Orthodox priest from West London should be passing through rural Hertfordshire, Cecil was too trusting a man to pay this oddity any heed. 'I'm glad you did, Father,' he said. 'I'll just finish up here, and then perhaps I can offer you a glass of sherry.'

'Excellent.'

Cecil examined his bunch of keys, selected one, and turned towards the vestry. As he did so, Grigorski took a cosh from his pocket and hit him over the head. The old man fell to the floor.

Kneeling down, Grigorski picked up the prone body as if it weighed nothing and threw it over his shoulder. Then he turned his steps to the clock tower.

# CHAPTER 8

## i

'I THOUGHT I'D CALL HIM JACK. An honest English name.'

'A Jack Russell called Jack... I'm sorry, Prime Minister, but you don't want to be accused of lacking imagination.'

The Prime Minister sighed. Natalie, though only twenty-six, had keener judgement than most of his special advisers. But she could be irritatingly pedantic.

'I suppose you want to put it to a focus group. Or perhaps an online vote would be more democratic.'

Natalie winced. 'There's no telling what that might produce. Much better that the call is yours.'

The Prime Minister gazed at the tiny bundle of fur asleep in the Harrods dog basket Oleg Ogorodnikov had sent him. There were moments when he hated being the one who had to make all the decisions.

Suddenly he had a brainwave.

'Bertrand!' he exclaimed. 'As in Bertrand Russell. Good

joke, don't you think?'

But Natalie still looked disapproving.

'It's not a very common name, is it?' she said. 'It might be considered elitist. Not to mention the fact that Russell was a philosopher: hardly an icon of instinctivism.'

'Well, then...suppose we shorten it to Bert. Nobody can object to that.'

'I think that would work very well, Prime Minister.'

Bert stirred luxuriously in his bed, as if conscious of his place on tomorrow's front pages.

'And now,' said Natalie, 'we need to think about your *Desert Island Discs*.'

ii

In another part of the city, Grigorski poured himself a cup of coffee, tore open a packet of shortbread biscuits with his teeth and returned to his listening post. The microphone in the dog basket was working well, though he could have done with less of the occupant's snuffling. What to make of this new conversation, though? What could the Prime Minister possibly mean by 'Chirpy Chirpy Cheep Cheep'?'

'The thing is, Ben, I think there's been a murder.'

Ben shook his head. 'I have to say, Anita, that I've never known a woman with a life as full of drama as yours. I suppose you're going to tell me that Oleg Ogorodnikov is involved.'

'I've no idea who is involved. But I'm absolutely certain that someone has blood on their hands.'

'Explain.'

'Don't listen to her!' came a voice from the kitchen. 'It's one of her nutcase conspiracy theories.'

'Oh do shut up, Esther!' Anita grimaced and mimed the act of strangulation.

The cavernous flat she shared with her sister occupied the basement of a house in Streatham. The sharing, however, took an unusual form.

The two rooms glimpsed on entering the hall were models of good order and traditional English taste. The furniture was antique; the fabrics were of floral chintz. Photographs in silver frames gleamed from mantelpieces and bookshelves; porcelain boxes with pictures of dogs, pheasants and foxes crowded the side tables. Nineteenth-century prints and framed samplers decorated the walls, while a teddy bear's head peeped from beneath a counterpane.

These, Anita had explained, were Esther's bedroom and sitting-room.

'Dad moved in here after my parents' divorce and started doing it up, but he ran out of money halfway through. Esther likes everything done and dusted, but I'm more relaxed, so when he died we agreed that we'd share the kitchen and bathroom, she'd take the other two rooms he'd finished, and I'd have the part he hadn't got to yet. As it's bigger than the rest put together, I think I've got rather a good deal.'

This was questionable. Though spacious, Anita's territory was far from comfortable. Carpets and rugs went only a small way towards hiding the great expanse of concrete floor, while the plaster on the walls still awaited a coat of paint. A battery of heaters stood in for radiators which had yet to be installed.

It was the contents, however, which first caught the eye. The fruits of Anita's salvage expeditions dominated: ancient doors stacked together like playing cards; austere pews; elaborately carved prie-dieux; tarnished lecterns and altar rails; battered pulpits; an entire reredos screen with flourishes as fine as lace; a baptismal font of old stone which must have required half a dozen men to shift it. Anything needed to furnish a church was, it seemed, here for the asking. Anita and Ben sat opposite each other in tall bishops' chairs with Latin inscriptions.

'Two days ago,' said Anita, 'a wonderful old clergyman called Cecil Simpson was found dead outside a church in Hertfordshire which he was temporarily looking after. According to the police, he had fallen from the bell tower – either because he'd had a dizzy spell, or because he'd jumped.

'But here's the thing: I knew Cecil pretty well. He was an expert on church architecture and he helped me with a couple of articles I wrote on the subject. And one thing he told me was that he suffered from vertigo. Nothing would induce him to go up a bell tower unless he absolutely had to.'

'So you think that someone forced him up there and then gave him a push?'

'It's the only explanation that makes sense.'

'But perhaps he did have an urgent reason to go up it, and having got to the top, was overcome by vertigo.'

'There's another thing, though: Cecil had problems with his knees. I don't believe he could have climbed the bell tower even if he wanted to.'

'Have you told this to the police?'

'I tried to. They said that I'd be surprised how many people can overcome physical disabilities in urgent situations – for example, if they want to kill themselves.'

'And you don't think it could have been suicide?'

'Absolutely not. Cecil's faith was as solid as a rock. He believed the Great Awakening was the beginning of a golden age of Christianity.'

'You said he was there temporarily. How long exactly?'

'He'd been there a month and was expecting to stay for a couple more.'

'So not really long enough to make a local enemy who would want to kill him?'

'That's what the police said. And I would agree. So it must have been someone who knew him beforehand and decided to follow him there.'

'But why, if he was such a wonderful old guy?'

'That's what we've got to find out.'

'We?'

'Yes. I saved your neck, remember? So I think you owe me a favour. Two heads are better than one.'

'You seem to be forgetting that I saved your neck first. Wouldn't it be best to wait and see what comes out of the inquest?'

'Absolutely not. The police say they have no reason to suspect foul play, so the church hasn't been secured as a crime scene. We need to get there before all the clues disappear – tomorrow if possible.'

'I told you not to listen to her,' said the voice from the kitchen. 'I hope you've got your own car. I wouldn't get into that God-awful van of hers if it was the last one on earth.'

## iv

'Will there be anything else, sir?'

'No,' said Ogorodnikov. 'Leave us.'

The waiter withdrew.

The evening was going exactly as the oligarch had planned. Here he was with the woman of his dreams – and how gorgeous she looked tonight! – dining tête-à-tête on the roof of his penthouse while a full moon rose obligingly overhead, bathing the classical statuary around them in its light.

'Another glass, my dear?'

'Why not?' She smiled her incomparable smile. Champagne splashed into the crystal flute; she raised it to her enticing lips.

'To you, Oleg,' she said.

'To you.'

Divorcing his wife would cost him millions – possibly

billions. Olga had been with him since the early days, when he was just a small-time black marketeer, and stuck by him through thick and thin; she had borne him three daughters. But despite all the expensive cosmetic surgery, she had lost her looks and become shrewish with it, growing increasingly resentful of his affairs. It was time for them to part; fortunately he had shared only a fraction of his business dealings with her, so there was little chance of her lawyers discovering the true extent of his fortune, or how Anton Ivanovich was exponentially increasing it.

But however much he had to pay out, it would be worth it for this young goddess, this exquisite minx. How sensational she would look at the state opening of Parliament – and afterwards in their bedroom, clad only in an ermine-trimmed robe. He felt sure, too, that she would do what Olga had failed to: bear him a male heir to his great empire.

For now, the only question was what film to show after dinner in his private cinema. *The Wizard of Oz? Pulp Fiction? E.T.?*

He smiled her. 'Have you got everything you want, my dear?' he asked.

'Yes, Oleg,' said Svetlana. 'I have.'

v

'Beautiful,' said Anita, surveying the interior of the ancient church with satisfaction. 'Just beautiful. Originally twelfth century, I'd say, judging from the crossing tower and that door at the west end; the rest of it looks fourteenth or fifteenth. Perpendicular at its best. And just look at the detail: the exquisite mediaeval glass in those tracery lights, the crocketed finials on the porch. A shame you can barely see the wall painting – those wretched Puritans and their whitewash. Problems with damp, of course, but in much better nick than many. Cecil Simpson must have loved it.'

'So he was a traditionalist?'

'None more so. You should have heard him on the subject of All God's Creatures' vandalism.' She breathed deeply to inhale the air, redolent of old hymn-books and dusty kneelers. 'All it lacks is a whiff of incense.'

'No chance of that here.' Ben paused to examine the plain wooden lectern. 'This is low church with a capital L. I doubt they've seen a censer since the Reformation.'

'The way up to the bell tower must be through that door.'

She was right. They found themselves climbing a steep, narrow stone staircase which eventually opened onto a forlorn space where floorboards of unsurpassed dustiness led to a cluster of bell ropes. The next opening revealed the belfry; the one above it, a door onto the parapet of the tower.

'There's no way Cecil could have got himself up here,' said Anita. 'Believe me.'

'If someone carried him up, they must have been very strong.'

'He was pretty skinny – he can't have weighed much. But yes, it would have been an effort.'

The mist which had clung to the fields on their drive from

London had yet to disperse, and the view from the tower was a limited one. For a moment Ben felt as if he were in the crow's nest of a ship becalmed on a grey ocean. But the ground below was clear enough, as was the damage a fall could do.

'The killer must have known the church well to come up with such a plan,' he said. 'So it looks like someone local after all.'

'Not necessarily – it could just have been a question of casing the joint.'

'So what do we do now? Try the police again?'

'We need something more to convince them. A clue they might have missed.'

Though Ben could not fault Anita's logic, he had a sense that she was living in the pages of a detective novel which remained closed to him. He look around half-heartedly, while keeping a firm grip on the parapet's lichened stone.

'I didn't see any footprints on the stairs,' he said.

'No, but there might be something.'

She set off around the base of the steeple. Ben followed. What could she possibly hope to find? Bloodstains?

'There!' she cried. She was leaning over the parapet, pointing at something that had caught on the back of a gargoyle's neck. 'It looks like a handkerchief. Maybe the killer dropped it and it got caught by a gust of wind. Can you reach it? You've got longer arms than I have.'

Ben hesitated. He was not particularly worried by heights, but a tower from which a man had recently fallen to his death was not to be taken lightly. The handkerchief might belong to anyone; unless it happened to have a nametape or embroidered initials on it, he would be risking his neck for very little reason.

'Come on,' said Anita impatiently.

Ben leant down. How far was he above the ground? A hundred feet? More?

'I don't think I can quite manage it,' he said.

'You're almost there. You just need to stretch a bit more. I'll hold on to your belt.'

The offer gave him little reassurance. But, obediently, he tried once more, straining his sinews. Finally two of his fingers closed over a corner of white cotton.

'Got it.'

He struggled to right himself; for a moment he swayed dangerously. Fortunately Anita's grip on his belt was strong.

'So,' he said, examining the handkerchief. 'No name, no initials – but how about this?' He pointed to a corner embroidered with five tiny Olympic rings and the words 'SOCHI 2014'. 'Perhaps there's been a ski-jumper up here. And this is strange,' he added, holding the handkerchief close to his nose.

'What?' asked Anita.

'Incense.'

## vi

To his surprise, Kevin enjoyed altering Alfred Wallis's paintings. It was tricky work, because the artist hadn't always left enough room for cats and dogs. But the challenge of adapting the composition, as well as imagining how Wallis would have presented the animals, felt far more satisfying than just making copies.

'Perhaps it's time for you to move on,' said Donna when he had submitted twelve paintings and Lyle St Ives had fast-tracked the exhibition. 'Have a go at something completely original.'

But Kevin shook his head. 'No,' he said. 'I'm nowhere near ready for that.'

*Ships' Cats and Sea Dogs* did not, to his relief, receive widespread attention. But it achieved its purpose, in that the visiting journalists were able to report that Lyle St Ives had embraced instinctivism in an exemplary manner.

'It's at the heart of everything we do,' Eldridge-Cattermole assured them. 'Art that does not engage with contemporary issues cannot be considered art at all. Wherever aesthetics and God's prior creations meet, Lyle St Ives is there in spirit.'

Donna received the Employee of the Month award.

'Very well done,' said Eldridge-Cattermole. 'Your friend Kevin – sorry, Scrawny Trelawny – has transformed Alfred Wallis's legacy.'

'He's very versatile,' said Donna. 'If you want the same done for any other artists… He's given me two incredibly convincing Picassos and a Monet.'

'Has he indeed?' said Eldridge-Cattermole. 'Good for him.'

'Hi, Pamela.'

'Hi, Auntie Jennifer.'

The two women were in the habit of meeting for lunch once a month at a café in central Oxford, close to Jennifer Pettifer's office in County Hall. She had always resented her glamorous sister Kate, but – to her surprise – felt a strong bond with Pamela, Kate's only child.

This was based in part on a shared suspicion of the world at large: a sense that people were out to cut corners and do them down, and must be brought to book for the public good. Jennifer, with no family of her own, had come to regard Pamela as a substitute daughter, and expressed the hope that she too might pursue a career in the civil service.

Disappointingly, Pamela had decided otherwise; but Jennifer had followed her progress through the lower ranks of academe with pride. Pamela, for her part, had been happy to accept Jennifer as a surrogate mother, whose job on the county council and passion for bureaucracy made her infinitely preferable as a role model to the flighty, fun-loving Kate.

'They've got tofu shepherd's pie as the dish of the day,' said Jennifer. 'I think I'll have that. But choose whatever you want.'

Pamela decided on a cauliflower steak. She didn't much like vegetarian food, but a champion of instinctivism could hardly eat meat in public. It was just one of those sacrifices life demanded.

'The Prime Minister seems to have seen the light,' she said. 'I'm happy to say that there's now a dog at 10 Downing Street.'

'Isn't it the sweetest thing? They were on the news together last night, welcoming the French president. Bert! What a wonderful choice of name.'

'Wonderful,' agreed Pamela.

'I thought I might knit him a little jacket – a Union Jack design with the letter B.'

'Wonderful.'

Their food arrived. The tofu shepherd's pie looked, if possible, even less appetising than the cauliflower steak.

'So how's everything going?' asked Jennifer.

'Very well. Almost too well, to tell the truth – I'm feeling rather overwhelmed by it all. We've been inundated with applications for the animal theology course: so much so that I've got to recruit three more lecturers. I should really be at Rickmansworth full time, but there's so much important work to do with the magazine.'

'Are you enjoying it a bit more?'

'I wouldn't call it enjoyable – but as I say, it's hugely important. I'm lucky that Alex Rosewater is so supportive: he's always got ideas for articles, and sends me lots we can reprint from American magazines. And the All God's Creatures social media team are terrific. You wouldn't believe how many followers we've got.'

'And the problems are?'

Pamela sighed. 'First of all, I really want to change the name of the magazine. *Cowthedral* would be so much more inclusive than *Cathedral*. But the marketing team have dug their heels in, and Alex agrees with them.

'Then there's a lot of pressure to give speeches and sound-bites for the cause. As you know, it's not really my thing. And then…'

'Then what?'

'There's this editorial assistant, Tamsin. She's a real fly in the ointment. She's not a member of All God's Creatures, and I'm sure she reports everything we discuss to that petphobic former editor. The trouble is that she's the only person who understands the whole production process. I certainly don't.'

Jennifer smiled and laid a hand on hers. 'No one is indispensable – believe me. I've got rid of any number of people who thought they had a job for life. We'll sort something out. Trust your Auntie Jennifer.'

### viii

Two days later Tamsin rang Ben.

'They're trying to get rid of me,' she said.

'How?'

'They're claiming that as a known associate of a petphobic writer my presence makes other members of the staff feel deeply uncomfortable.'

'Which writer is this?'

'You.'

'But I'm not petphobic. I loved Molly – that's what started

all this.'

'You're using something they're not interested in, Ben – common sense.'

'So who exactly is deeply uncomfortable? If you're my known associate, so is everyone else who's worked for *Cathedral* in the last ten years.'

'Not quite: we've got a new intern. Some relation of Dr Pettifer's, I think.'

'And he or she lives in terror of anyone who's ever met me?'

'Apparently.'

'That would never hold water at an employment tribunal.'

'It might, the way things are going.'

'But you're the lynchpin of the magazine, Tamsin. They can't do without you.'

'My guess is that they've got a team set up in America. An awful lot of our material is coming from there now.'

'But…you can't just let *Cathedral* become a mouthpiece for a foreign pressure group.'

'It's pretty much that already. And what can I do to stop it?'

Ben thought for a moment.

'You need to do some snooping,' he said.


ix


The first chapter of *A Lot To Look Forward To* was a cracker, if Anton said so himself. It opened in a lonely country churchyard where Pip, the hero, was visiting his parents' graves. Suddenly an escaped convict jumped out from behind a tombstone and threatened to kill him if he didn't bring him food and a file to get rid of his chains. But Pip outsmarted him and went straight to the police, who arrested the man and took him back to prison, swearing revenge as he went. What form would that revenge take? That was the question…

# CHAPTER 9

## i

BEN NEEDED SOME COAXING to join Hughie on another boat trip: the memory of the corpse they had found floating in the river was all too vivid. But Hughie persuaded him that it was necessary.

'Like getting back on a horse after you've had a fall,' he said. 'Unless you do it quickly, you might never want to again.'

For Ben, there was an extra incentive: the opportunity to discuss Anita's suspicions without any danger of being overheard.

The outing got off to a rough start. A sudden squall blew up as they left Westminster Pier; rain lashed at the windows of the small cabin, and Hughie's horse-riding analogy seemed all too apt as the vessel bucked and reared between troughs of water. But just as quickly, the wind died down, the rain-clouds lifted, and sunlight stretched across the river as if to ask what all the fuss had been about.

'A handkerchief smelling of incense?' said Hughie when Ben had told the story of his visit to Hertfordshire. 'It's not exactly incontrovertible evidence. Even if it had blood on it, you'd be struggling to make a case.'

'But incense is more interesting than blood – in this case, anyway. It means the murderer has a connection to another church: Catholic, high Anglican or Orthodox. You have to admit that it's an unusual scenario.'

'A bit too unusual. There's no proof that a murder has actually been committed; or, if it has been, that the snot rag had anything to do with it. No one who hadn't worked on Britain's top ecumenical magazine would seriously be wondering which denomination might be responsible. I think your head's been turned by this Anita girl. What's she like, anyway? Drop-dead gorgeous, I suspect.'

'You've seen her, actually. She was the one who threw the boeuf Stroganoff at Ogorodnikov.'

'For God's sake, Ben!' Hughie gave him an incredulous look. 'That girl is trouble, believe me – I've known all too many like her. As your godfather and your employer, I'm telling you to have nothing more to do with her.'

'But like I said, she saved my skin. I can't very well refuse to help her.'

'You've already repaid her by going along with her detective fantasy.'

'I don't believe it *is* a fantasy. I climbed to the top of that bell tower, and Anita's right – there's no way an elderly man with dodgy knees and vertigo would have gone up there of his own free will.'

Hughie sighed. 'Well, that looks like Aziz up ahead. Try your theory on him, if you must.'

He steered towards the police launch.

'Morning, Aziz!' he called as they drew alongside. 'Any news on that body we found?'

Aziz shook his head. 'Not to speak of. His wife identified the body. No obvious reason for suicide, or anything else. We're just waiting for the inquest.'

'Ben here has something he'd like to tell you about. Have you got a moment?'

'Of course.'

Aziz listened attentively to Ben's story.

'The idea of the elderly gentleman climbing to that height certainly seems odd,' he said. 'But as the local force told your friend, people can do extraordinary things in extraordinary circumstances. Let's suppose there was a crime, though. Did your friend suggest a motive?'

'No,' Ben admitted.

'Then it's difficult. I do have a mate up in Hertfordshire, and I could suggest that he take another look, but I'm pretty sure what the answer would be. Most forces are overstretched at the moment, what with the All God's Creatures demonstrations and the petphobic hate crimes.'

'What about the handkerchief? Could you do a DNA test on it?'

Aziz shrugged. 'There's a big backlog at the labs as well. Unless there's a better reason to believe that it would tell us something...'

Then, seeing the disappointment on Ben's face, he

relented. 'But look, after the help you gave us the other day, I can at least ask my mate. I'll let you know what he says.'

'You're very kind.'

'Not a problem.'

And with a wave of his hand, Aziz was gone.

## ii

Ben had read reports of All God's Creatures demonstrations, but it was not until he and Hughie disembarked at Westminster Pier that he witnessed one for himself. When he did, he was astonished.

The streets around Westminster Abbey and the Houses of Parliament had been half-empty two hours earlier; now they teemed with people. Demonstrators young and old had congregated, many waving colourful banners, some wheeling children in pushchairs. 'Instinctivism now!' they chanted. 'Archbishop out!'

And with them they had brought their animals. These were dogs for the most part – Ben noticed a beautiful golden retriever which could almost have been Molly in her prime. There were also at least a dozen horses; a handful of alpacas; a couple of cows; the odd sheep; half a dozen different kinds of poultry. One shaven-headed young woman had a python curled around her neck and shoulders.

'Blimey,' said Hughie. 'This is what I call a demo. I haven't see anything like it since the Countryside Alliance marches.'

Ben's only thought was that if anyone recognised him, he would be torn limb from limb. He needed to get away from the throng, but he was hemmed in on every side. He reached for his sunglasses and pulled his cap down low over his forehead.

The crowds were generally well disciplined, with stewards in yellow 'AGC' tabards directing the march. But on the fringes there were signs of trouble.

'Better watch out for that lot,' said Hughie, indicating a group of black-clad anarchists. 'There's nothing they like better than spoiling a party.'

But Ben's gaze was fixed on the next street corner, where a small but noisy collection of Young Humanists were mounting a counter-demonstration.

'Animals are for eating! Man is the measure of all things!' they yelled.

Half a dozen tough-looking men broke away from the procession to confront them. To Ben's surprise, the toughest one looked familiar.

'That bloke in the green jacket,' he said, nudging Hughie. 'It's Ogorodnikov's bodyguard – the one who got on the wrong end of the boeuf Stroganoff.'

'Very odd. I wouldn't have had him down as an animal-lover – or a church-goer.'

As he spoke, the bodyguard head-butted the nearest Young Humanist, who fell to the pavement.

The mêlée spread with extraordinary swiftness. The body-guard shouted with pain as a goat butted him squarely on the knee; his nearest companion tumbled on top of him, felled by a Young Humanist placard; two stewards waded in, only to find themselves wrestling with plain-clothes policemen; an alpaca spat at a uniformed officer. Soon several dozen people were trading blows, with a cacophony of animal noises adding to the confusion.

But just as the situation seemed completely out of control, a hush fell on the crowd. The gates of the House of Commons swung open, and an instantly recognisable figure emerged: the Prime Minister, preceded by a small dog on an orange lead, and followed by a phalanx of protection officers.

'Champions of your fellow creatures,' he declared as the ranks of demonstrators parted before him like the Red Sea before Moses, 'your government has heard you. We will work with you to build a truly instinctivist society. No churchman will stand in our way. To Lambeth Palace!'

'To Lambeth Palace!' The cry spread across Parliament Square like a surfer's wave hurrying towards Malibu. The Prime Minister set off along Millbank; in front of him, Bert strained at his leash like a valiant tugboat towing a giant cruise ship out to sea. The crowd followed.

### iii

Fortunately for the Archbishop of Canterbury, Natalie had given him advance warning. He and his wife were already in their small electric car, nosing through the mean streets of south London, though worried that the battery might give out before they reached Canterbury.

'I told you that you should have excommunicated them,' said his wife.

The archbishop sighed. She was right, as usual. And now it was too late – he couldn't do it without losing half the young curates in the country. A schism would surely follow. He would have liked to excommunicate the Prime Minister as well, but a rupture between Church and State was the last thing he needed.

He prayed that the doors of Lambeth Palace would keep the mob out. Natalie had explained that the Prime Minister would make a show of trying to gain entry and then – having established his credentials with the crowd – persuade everyone to disperse. Still, it was time to think about upgrading security. He wondered if the Pope might lend him some Swiss Guards.

iv

In a café behind Westminster Abbey, Alex Rosewater's phone rang.

'I think everything has gone according to plan,' said the voice at the other end. 'Time to move on to the next phase.'

# CHAPTER 10

i

'I NEED YOU TO MAKE A DELIVERY,' said Ezra Cairns. 'That big harbour scene by Julia Collis.'

'Bet I know who's bought it,' said Kevin. 'That couple who were in on Saturday.'

'Wrong: a woman from Bristol. She does sets for TV and reckons it would look just right in a new series she's working on.'

'So you want me to drive to Bristol?'

'No, no. She's staying near St Just and is about to head home. She doesn't have time to come into St Ives, so you're to meet her on the road to hand it over. She's sent something called a GPS position which I don't understand but I hope you will.

*If there's something that's all Greek to me*
*It's new, new, new technology!*

Kevin was relieved. He felt comfortable driving around

the Cornish byways, but Bristol and the major roads leading to it…in his imagination they felt like another world. He'd found his patch and was happy to stick to it.

'I won't be using the van this evening,' Ezra added, 'so no need to hurry back. You could take that girl of yours for a scenic drive and propose to her at Land's End.'

Kevin laughed. 'She'd turn me down flat as a pancake. Anyway, she's off at a hen party in London.'

'Well, any time you want to borrow my romantic automobile for that particular purpose…'

Kevin checked the GPS co-ordinates. The place was only ten miles away, just the other side of Pendeen, but the road was a slow one – twisty and narrow. He'd allow forty minutes, just to be safe. Maybe he'd stop for a drink at Gurnard's Head on the way back.

It was late afternoon when he loaded the bubble-wrapped painting into the back of the van and set off. The sun, beginning its descent into the ocean, was in his eyes as he followed the coast road west, but it was only a minor irritation. He loved the landscape at this time of day, with the light softening the open fields and glinting on the sea. How much he had missed, growing up in the city! He smiled at the sight of a group of ponies on the hillside, staring down upon him.

'Perhaps I could learn to ride,' he thought: 'become a real countryman.'

He reached the rendezvous ten minutes early. He'd imagined a lay-by, but found himself instead at the entrance to something called the Geevor Tin Mine Museum – or at least, at the entrance of a small road leading down to it. It was a good spot for a quick handover: the customer could draw up beside him and be on her way in a minute.

He googled the tin mine while he was waiting. The statistics were awesome: by the time it was shut down in 1990, eighty-five miles of tunnels had been dug and fifty thousand tons of tin removed. The biggest challenge had been emptying it of water: over a million gallons had to be pumped out daily. The museum was closed now, but maybe he'd come back for a proper look-see. He wondered if Donna would be interested; perhaps it was more of a bloke thing.

The customer was late. That was odd, given how tight her schedule was and how precise she'd been about the rendezvous. Still, you never knew with these country roads: she could literally be stuck behind a herd of cows. He wondered if Ezra had given her his number.

His phone rang.

'Where are you?' a woman's voice demanded.

'I'm at the meeting place. I've been here for twenty minutes. Where are you?'

'In the car park. Don't tell me your boss told you to wait on the road.'

'He just gave me the GPS position. He didn't mention a car park.'

'Well, get yourself down here. Head down towards the main building and you'll find it easily enough. I haven't got all day.'

Kevin followed the patched tarmac driveway down towards the sea. The collection of buildings ahead of him looked bleak and largely abandoned; it certainly wasn't like any museum he'd been taken to as a boy. A huge, weird triangular steel structure, like half an electricity pylon, dominated a motley collection of buildings: some concrete, some brick; some with tiled roofs, some with mossy corrugated ones. There were rusted fuel tanks and ancient pieces of machinery; there were steel fences and tumbledown walls. Only a coat of bright blue paint on the reception area suggested that the complex was still in use.

The car park lay in the shelter of a large mound of earth. The single other vehicle to be seen was a black SUV.

Kevin parked beside it and walked round to the back of the van. As he did so, a man and a woman climbed out of the car. The man was holding a gun.

'Hello, Kevin,' he said. 'We've got some business to discuss.'

## ii

'Who are you?' asked Kevin. 'What do you want?'

'You can call me Clyde. And my associate – well, why not Bonnie? That OK with you, love?'

'Fine by me,' said the woman.

They were a strange-looking couple. Clyde was a small, skinny man with straggly black hair down to his shoulders. The woman was several inches taller and looked as if she had just emerged from a beauty salon, her blonde hair immaculate and her face shiny with make-up. While Clyde was dressed entirely in distressed denim, she wore a pristine raincoat and creaseless suede boots.

'As for what we want,' Clyde continued: 'your skills, Kev. We hear you're very handy with a paintbrush.'

Kevin was more mystified than ever.

'Who'd you hear that from?'

Clyde laughed. 'That's for us to know and you to wonder. But you come very highly recommended. There's nothing you can't copy, apparently: Picasso, Alfred Wallis, Gauguin…'

'I've never copied a Gauguin.'

'But you could, couldn't you? You've got the eye; you'd soon learn the technique. Our friend says you can turn your hand to anything.'

'Van Gogh,' said Bonnie. 'That's what we've got in mind for you. A very beautiful still life.'

'I don't get it,' said Kevin. 'If you just want me to copy a painting, why are you pointing a shooter at me?'

'Because you're a known associate of a convicted murderer,' said Clyde. 'Can't be too careful. But as a gesture of good will…'

He lowered the gun and tucked it into the waistband of his jeans.

'And why ask me anyway?' Kevin went on. 'Why not just order a copy off the internet?'

'Because it's got to pass for the real thing.'

'You mean…you want to try and *sell* it?'

'You're beginning to get the picture,' said Clyde, 'if you'll pardon the pun.'

'The painting is called *Poppy Flowers*,' said Bonnie. 'It disappeared from a museum in Cairo in 2010 and no one has seen it since.'

'So you want to pretend you've found it and claim the reward? Forget it. They'd have the top experts in the world to look at it. Even if I did a brilliant copy, they'd check the paint, they'd check the canvas… There's no way it'd get past them.'

'You'll have plenty of back-up. We've got experts of our own. They'll supply the right paint and a convincing canvas. In any case, we won't be taking it to a museum. Who wants a reward when you can get the full price?'

'What, from a bent collector?'

'Maybe a collector,' said Clyde. 'Or…there are people who use paintings as currency: easy to move about, none of the aggravation of nosy bank managers. They're insurance, too: any villain the law catches up with can say, "Go easy on me and I can tell you where to find a lost masterpiece."'

'But they'd check it too. They'd have their own experts.'

'Not in the same way,' said Bonnie. 'How many Van Gogh scholars are going to risk their reputations by authenticating a stolen picture? All we need from you is something good enough for our purposes – and we're confident you can deliver.'

'It'll be a nice little earner for you too,' said Clyde. 'Maybe you'll be able to buy some wheels of your own. Then you won't have to borrow that poxy van.'

'And if I say no…you'll shoot me?'

'I don't think we'd have to do that,' said Clyde. 'Big Mario's still locked up, but his brother Gino is out, and he'd be very interested to know your whereabouts – no two ways about it. And if you're thinking of doing a runner, forget it: we'll be watching you.'

# CHAPTER 11

### i

PAMELA PETTIFER WAS MAKING such heavy weather of her editorial that in the end Alex Rosewater had to dictate it to her. Perched on the edge of her desk swinging his legs, he looked more than ever like a schoolboy playing truant.

'Much good work has been done in preparing the interiors of outmoded churches for universal Communion,' he intoned. 'Pews have been removed, doorways widened, stabling areas created. But the quest for justice cannot stop there. Many churches remain which are, in their entirety, an affront to all right-thinking people. And none of them inspire greater abhorrence than the 24 London churches attributed to Sir Christopher Wren.

'More than any other architect in history, Wren had the opportunity to accommodate all God's creatures. Charged with rebuilding the city's churches after the Great Fire of 1666, he could have effected the changes in layout so belatedly being made. Instead, he chose to perpetuate the privilege of the traditional elite.

'History has been too kind to Wren. It is time to call out his prejudice. *Cathedral* demands that he be posthumously stripped of his knighthood and that the churches he designed be demolished, to be replaced with worship spaces suited to a more enlightened age.'

## ii

'It couldn't happen, could it?' said Mrs Petrovna. 'All those beautiful churches…it would be vandalism! And sacrilege!'

'It shouldn't be possible,' said Ben. 'Of course not. But in the present climate you can't be certain of anything.'

'Surely the heritage people would block it without a second thought,' said Svetlana.

'They might have once. But now they tend to go whichever way the political wind blows.'

'So who can stop it?'

'There's a meeting of the Church of England's general synod next week, and it will be discussed there. That will give some indication of what to expect. But ultimately it's up to the Church Commissioners.'

Mrs Petrovna shook her head. 'It couldn't happen in the Orthodox Church. Not in a thousand years.'

'Hasn't it had any pressure from All God's Creatures?'

'Some of their people turned up outside the cathedral one

Sunday, but they soon realised they weren't going to get anywhere. I'm afraid some of the parishioners may have been a little rough with them.'

Ben had met many devout people, but none whose attachment to their place of worship surpassed his landlady's. Every day, come rain or shine, she set off for the cathedral – if not to attend a service, then to help with the cleaning or comfort the down-and-outs who came to its doors. 'Saintly' did not seem too strong a word. And yet she had her finger firmly on the pulse of the material world, keeping the radio permanently tuned to the BBC, reading the *Daily Telegraph* from cover to cover, and providing him with summaries of the latest current affairs programmes. At the same time, she delighted in whatever gossip came out of Chicane.

'I used only to get it from Svetlana,' she said. 'But now I get it from both of you – why, it's like listening in stereo.'

Ben found her company delightful. She was, moreover, an excellent cook, eager to feed him whenever they coincided at mealtimes. Today being Sunday, she had prepared a sublime leg of lamb with dauphinoise potatoes and home-made redcurrant jelly; and since the phrase 'second helping' was clearly not part of Svetlana's vocabulary, he felt duty-bound to accept whatever her grandmother heaped on his plate.

It was while Mrs Petrovna was in the kitchen that he told Svetlana about his sighting of Ogorodnikov's bodyguard.

'That *is* surprising,' Svetlana said. 'Still, I suppose what bodyguards get up to in their spare time is their own business. If he'd been marching in favour of expelling all foreigners, I suppose it would have been of some concern.'

'You must know Ogorodnikov pretty well, since he's such a valued member of the club.'

'No, not really. I know what he wants from Chicane, of course, but I get all that from his P.A. And whenever he comes, he's with a crowd of friends. I've never actually talked to him one-to-one.'

Mrs Petrovna returned with three flawless rum babas.

'By the way, Ben,' she said, 'I wonder if I might ask you a favour. There's a new priest at the cathedral – he hasn't been in England very long, and I don't think he's got to know many people. I feel that the least I can do is invite him to tea. But I'm afraid it would be very boring for him just having me to talk to, and Svetlana is always very busy in the afternoon. Would you mind very much if I roped you in to meet him?'

'I don't think he'd find you boring for a moment,' said Ben. 'But of course I'd be delighted.'

'Thank you, dear. I'll find a date you can both manage. His name is Father Peter.'


### iii


Mrs Petrovna's invitation was the last thing Grigorski wanted. He had little enough time to himself, what with Moscow's demands and the appearances he had to put in at the cathedral. In all probability he would have to give up his weekly poker game with the embassy's military attaché. But the Petrovna woman was damnably persistent and held in high regard by the Metropolitan; he could not refuse her without jeopardising his cover. And so, reluctantly, he accepted.


## iv


Ben got a phone call from Inspector Aziz.

'Sorry, Mr Fairweather,' the policeman said. 'I spoke to my mate in Hertfordshire, but he said he couldn't help. They've just got too much on their plate to act on a vague hypothesis – his words, not mine. I did my best, but there it is.'

'That's very disappointing – but thank you for trying.'

'No problem. One other thing that might interest you – the inquest on that bloke you found for us is coming up. I'll send you the details.'


## v


Tamsin rang Ben to report on her research into Pamela Pettifer's past.

'I've got her like a rat in a trap,' she said when she had finished.

'Well, well. And what are you planning to do with this information? Confront her in the office?'

'After the way she's treated me? Relying on me to bring the magazine out week after week and then kicking me in the teeth? No, I'm going nuclear. She's been invited to appear on tonight's edition of that political discussion programme, *I'm Very Clear On This*. I happen to know one of the researchers. Don't miss it.'


## vi


Kevin found Van Gogh easier than he had expected. Yes, *Poppy Flowers* had a huge amount of detail – dozens of blooms bunched together in a vase – but once he'd got the hang of the broad brush strokes, he found himself moving fluently from one flower to the next. It helped that Bonnie and Clyde had provided him with an ultra-high-definition copy of the original, and a detailed analysis of which coloured oils were used where; in the end, though, it was instinct that guided his hand. At times he felt as if he had *become* Van Gogh, filled with the excitement of creating a masterpiece.

When he put down his brush, however, the awfulness of his situation left him almost paralysed. One moment he'd been living in paradise – in a place he loved with a girl he loved; the next he'd been dragged back into the dark world of Big Mario. It had been OK back then – at least until Big Mario fired the gun – because he hadn't known any better; but now, having glimpsed what life could be…it was more than he could bear.

His first thought had been to tell the witness protection officer. It didn't take long, though, to work out what she'd say: 'Your cover's blown – we've got to move you on.' It would be goodbye to St Ives, goodbye to Ezra, goodbye to Donna. He'd have to go through the whole business again, starting out in a new town, friendless, hopeless.

He desperately wanted to tell Donna – but then it would all come out. He'd spun the same yarn for her as for everyone else: he'd grown up in Norwich, got thrown out of home because he didn't get on with his mum's new boyfriend, and headed for Cornwall because it was as far as you could go. What would she do if she found out that he'd been lying to her all along – that he was there because he'd been involved in a gangland murder? She'd walk out on him: of course she would.

So he had no choice in the matter. He'd grit his teeth, do the painting as quickly as he could, and hope that it would satisfy Bonnie and Clyde. And with luck that would be that.

## vii

Jennifer Pettifer's day at the council offices had been routine; but being a woman who enjoyed routine, she felt perfectly fulfilled. She had chaired a committee on raising revenue by introducing parking restrictions where none were needed, and fine-tuned a proposal to make residents responsible for their own street-cleaning. Now she was looking forward to her niece's appearance on a prime-time TV show. She settled down on her sofa with a glass of Prosecco and several soft toys from her impressive collection.

The opening credits swirled across the screen like exotic fish in an aquarium; percussive music rose to a crescendo. Finally a host of disjointed letters resolved themselves into the words I'M VERY CLEAR ON THIS.

Of the three panellists, Pamela looked the most nervous – as well she might, with a live audience in front of her as well as the thousands of viewers at home. But she also looked very smart and very beautiful – altogether more attractive than the frumpy woman hosting the show.

The two other panellists were both men: a pallid clergyman and a perspiring expert on animal psychology. The show followed a long-established format of introducing and putting two questions to each guest before opening the debate to the whole panel. Tonight's subject, blazoned across the wall, was 'Animals: holier than thou?'

The frumpy host was friendly enough as she questioned the psychologist and the clergyman. Then she turned to Pamela.

'As Chief Word Organising Officer of *Cathedral*, Pamela Pettifer has taken a sleepy, niche magazine and placed it firmly at the heart of the national conversation. It is to all intents and purposes the voice of the phenomenon known as All God's Creatures. Its editorials make headline news, and its social media followers total seventeen million.

'Pamela Pettifer also holds the chair of animal theology at the University of Rickmansworth. Indeed, remarkably, she had no journalistic experience before becoming editor of *Cathedral*. But those who have queried her qualifications for the job have had to eat their words.

'However –' she paused for dramatic effect '– these are not the only qualifications to raise questions. We've been looking at Pamela Pettifer's CV, and discovered some strange discrepancies.'

She turned from the audience to face Pamela full-on.

'You claim, Ms Pettifer, to have a first-class bachelor's degree in sociology from Sussex University, a masters in marketing from Salford University and a doctorate in psychology from Aberdeen University. But we've checked the records of the institutions in question, and this is what we found. Your so-called first in sociology was actually a third; you failed your masters; and your doctorate was withdrawn following accusations of plagiarism. Isn't it true to say, then, that you are an out-and-out fraud?'

The audience's excitement was palpable. This was more than they could ever have hoped for: trial by television! In her flat, Jennifer lowered her glass of Prosecco in dismay.

For a moment it looked as if Pamela might burst into tears. Her fingers closed on her microphone as if she were about to tear it from her lapel and run from the studio. But then her face hardened into a mask of pure resolve.

'You're right about there being a discrepancy,' she said. 'But am I ashamed of it? No. The fact is that I had no choice in the matter. Because you know as well as I do that we live in a corrupt, elitist society that privileges human intelligence above all the other gifts in God's creation. As long as that's the case, people with high IQs will always rise to the top; and until we reverse that state of affairs, I believe that I – like everyone else – am entitled to subvert this shameful status quo.'

The camera panned across the audience's faces. Had she won their sympathy? The answer soon became clear.

'Instinctivism now!' came a shout from the back.

The cry was taken up by a hundred voices.

'All God's Creatures! Instinctivism now!'

Pamela smiled. Jennifer gave a deep sigh of relief and raised her glass to the screen.

## viii

'How could that idiot interviewer have let her get away with it?' thought Tamsin. 'Bloody hell!'

'Sleepy, niche magazine indeed,' thought Ben. 'Bloody hell!'

'Attagirl, Pammy!' thought Alex Rosewater, opening a bottle of something very much more expensive than Prosecco. 'A slam dunk if ever there was one. Here we go!'

# CHAPTER 12

i

'THERE'S SOMEONE HERE to see you, Quentin,' said Donna.
'Who?'

'Marina Bright.'

Eldridge-Cattermole looked up in alarm. What on earth was the Lyle's longest-serving trustee doing in St Ives? Why hadn't he been warned? His mind raced over all the things she might find fault with – and which it was now too late to do anything about.

True to her name, his visitor favoured a wardrobe of vibrant colours. Today she wore a raspberry-pink coat with a turquoise scarf and yellow patent-leather ankle boots. Large green spectacles perched on her nose beneath a fringe of white hair.

'Marina!' Eldridge-Cattermole ushered her into his office with feigned enthusiasm. 'To what do we owe this unexpected pleasure?'

'I'm staying with friends near Helston – a last-minute invitation. And of course, I couldn't miss the chance of paying you a visit. Besides which, I wanted to give you a heads-up.'

Eldridge-Cattermole blenched. This sounded ominous.

'The director of Lyle Britain is stepping down,' she said, 'for reasons I am not at liberty to divulge. I'm here to tell you, unofficially, that if you were to throw your hat into the ring, your application would be looked upon very favourably. I can't promise anything, but we've been very impressed by what you've done with limited resources to advance the instinctivist agenda. *Redeeming Alfred Wallis* was a brilliant idea – and there are any number of artists you could redeem at Lyle Modern.

'My advice to you is to keep up the good work. If you could do something equally imaginative with Barbara Hepworth's studio, that would be extremely helpful to your cause.'

## ii

Elated, but careful to keep the reason to himself, Eldridge-Cattermole called a meeting.

'Cats,' he said. 'That's the way to go, given that Hepworth was a felinophile.' He smiled at his coinage. 'Half a dozen of them as a permanent fixture? We could get the Leach Pottery to design bowls for them in collaboration with leading Cornish artists.'

'No cat is a permanent fixture,' said Ines, the deputy

director. 'One whiff of fish from the harbour and they'd be gone in a moment.'

Eldridge-Cattermole frowned. Ines had been a wet blanket ever since the plug had been pulled on her seagull Jackson Pollock exhibition – as if that had somehow been his fault. Wretched woman!

'Sheep, then,' he said. 'There's plenty of room for a couple in the garden – and no chance of them escaping.'

'You'd have the problem of the lanolin line,' said Alisa, the senior curator.

'What on earth is that?'

'It happens when the sheep rub themselves against sculptures: they destroy the patina, so the surface of the parts they can reach looks different from the parts they can't. It's caused the Henry Moore Foundation a lot of problems.'

'But that would be brilliant! God's prior creations responding to and embellishing human artefacts.'

'I'm not sure the trustees would see it that way – or the insurers.'

'I suppose you're right.' Eldridge-Cattermole sighed. 'Any other ideas?'

'Hamsters,' said Damien, the intern. He was a tall, self-confident young man with front teeth suggestive of the rodents in question. 'You could have a run for them with miniature versions of her sculptures. They'd love popping through all them holes.'

'Runs are cruel,' said Donna. 'It would be against the whole spirit of instinctivism.'

'For God's sake!' Suddenly Ros, the sculpture curator, was

on her feet gazing furiously at her colleagues. 'In case you've forgotten, we're talking about one of the greatest artists of the twentieth century. The fact that she liked cats is totally irrelevant to her work. You should just…just…treat her with more respect!'

'There's no disrespect here,' said Eldridge-Cattermole in his coldest voice. 'It's her respect for God's prior creations that we're celebrating, that's all.'

'Well, you can leave me out of it!'

Ros hurried from the room, slamming the door. The rest of the committee exchanged amused glances. Eldridge-Cattermole passed Donna a note: *Pls find me Ros's employment contract.*

'Actually,' said Ines, 'I think I've got the answer. What about that young Brazilian artist called Koribo who does amazing installations with enormous balloons? "Koribo's Incorrigible Dirigibles" he calls them. I think we should commission him to do one of Barbara Hepworth's cat and fly it over her studio. It would be really edgy – and a great photo opp.'

'Let's have a look,' said Eldridge-Cattermole.

They reached for their phones. Among the images summoned up were a Roman helmet floating above the amphitheatre in Nîmes and a golden heart beside the Taj Mahal. What the work lacked in subtlety, it more than made up for in scale.

'Excellent,' said Eldridge-Cattermole. 'Will you action that, Ines? As a matter or urgency, please.'

## iii

The last person Ben expected to find propping up the bar at Chicane was Sister Theodosia. But there she was, clinking whisky glasses with Hughie.

'Ben!' exclaimed Hughie. 'You've pitched up at exactly the right moment. Look who's decided to drop by.'

'Do you two know each other?' asked Ben.

'Oh yes,' said Sister Theodosia with a broad smile. 'We go way back.'

'Theodosia used to run a shebeen in Nairobi,' said Hughie. 'I spent many a happy evening there in my misspent youth.'

'This was before I found the Lord, you understand,' said Sister Theodosia. 'And Hughie – he was one handsome young man; but wild, oh yes! The idea that he could become someone's godfather...'

'The idea that you could become a nun...'

She laughed. 'The Lord moves in mysterious ways. Anyway, Ben, Tamsin was telling me about your new life, and I looked up Chicane on the internet and put two and two together – so I decided I'd come and see how you were getting on next time I was in London. And I'm glad I did. After a day at the General Synod, a glass of firewater is exactly what I need.'

'You were there?' said Ben. 'For the debate on the Wren churches?'

'Indeed I was.'

'And? What happened?'

'The vote was split 50-50. So now it's up to the Church Commissioners. But as there are several vacancies on the committee in question, it's hard to know which way it will go. It was a fierce debate, I can tell you. The Archbishop of Canterbury didn't look at all well by the end of it. There was actually a bit of a fracas.'

'What kind of a fracas?'

'It began with a speech by one of the financial officers, who said the Church was tightening its belt and couldn't possibly afford to demolish twenty-four churches and replace them with new ones. There was no mention of St Paul's Cathedral, you'll be relieved to hear – I'm not sure why. Anyway, then one of the All God's Creatures people got up and said a Russian philanthropist had made a very generous offer to cover the entire cost of demolition and rebuilding. All he wanted in return was to put a few flats above each of the new worship spaces.'

'Did they mention the philanthropist's name?' asked Hughie.

'Yes: it was Lord Ogorodnikov. That's when the trouble started. This young woman – I think she was a journalist – seized the microphone and started telling everyone that Ogorodnikov was the devil incarnate. A couple of security men came on to remove her, but she kicked and screamed like nobody's business. I think the police were called in the end.'

'This young woman,' said Ben. 'Was she quite small, with black curly hair tied in a very loud bandana?'

'Yes,' said Sister Theodosia.

'Oh Lord,' said Ben.

## iv

'You're generosity itself, Oleg,' said Svetlana. 'I can't imagine the cost of demolishing all those old churches. And all you're going to get in return is a few flats. How ridiculous that anyone should begrudge you those!'

Ogorodnikov smiled. 'I am glad to be of help. I have always been fond of animals: it is no exaggeration to say that Misha, my grandmother's Pekinese, taught me the meaning of love. But between you and me, my motives were not entirely selfless.'

'What do you mean?'

'The churches will be demolished, yes, but not disposed of. They will be rebuilt brick by brick in my wedding parks.'

'Wedding parks?'

'I am creating four of them – one outside Moscow and three in China. It is big business over there. People want to have their ceremonies and photographs and parties against a romantic backdrop – and what could be more romantic than a seventeenth-century London church? There will be half a dozen in each park, and Anton Ivanovich is certain that they will be booked up at least two years in advance.'

'You seem to have a lot of faith in that young man.'

Ogorodnikov smiled again. 'He is the best in the business, no doubt about it. I am very proud of him.'

'But Oleg, wouldn't it be cheaper just to build copies of the churches?'

'Cheaper, yes. But what people want these days is authenticity. That is why so many Chinese travel to Europe to buy designer goods: they do not want their friends to think they can only afford counterfeit Louis Vuitton, so they come here to be photographed with their purchases outside the London store. With real Wren churches we can charge ten times what we could for imitations. And Svetlana…'

'Yes, Oleg?'

'Perhaps you and I…'

Svetlana giggled. 'Oh Oleg,' she said. 'You old romantic!'

## v

'I'll kill him,' said Anita. 'I mean it. Even if I have to spend the rest of my life in prison, it'll be worth it to rid the world of that grasping philistine.'

'Please, Anita, calm down,' said Ben. He was standing at a discarded lectern in her flat, imagining himself reading the lesson to bewhiskered men and whaleboned women in a Victorian church. 'You were lucky the police let you off with a caution after the synod. If you're going to put an end to Ogorodnikov's machinations, you need a cool head. And whatever you do, I don't want to be traipsing out to some far-off prison every week to visit you.'

'You'd do that?'

'Well, yes. I'd want to make sure that you had enough books to read and weren't fomenting riots.'

As he spoke the words, however, he realised that there was more to it than that. Anita was not the kind of woman who normally attracted him, but there was something inescapably sexy about her fighting spirit. Might the two of them possibly…?

Before he could consider the subject further, she kissed him.

**vi**

'Now that,' said Clyde, 'is what I call a nice piece of work: very nice indeed. I don't know that Vincent himself could have told the difference. What do you think, Bonnie?'

'I think you're right,' said Bonnie, examining the brush-work through a magnifying glass. 'First rate – no doubt about it.'

Much as he wished he had never met his two visitors, Kevin couldn't help feeling a glow of pride. Copying Van Gogh had been a step up from copying Alfred Wallis, Picasso or even Monet – but he'd pulled it off. If only his *Poppy Flowers* could be shown on the walls of Lyle St Ives! Now, he imagined, it would vanish from sight for ever.

Clyde took a thick roll of notes from his pocket.

'This is for you, young man,' he said. 'You've earned it.'

For a moment Kevin was tempted. After all, he'd simply painted a copy to oblige one of Ezra's customers; he wasn't going to be the one passing it off as the real thing. But then he shook his head. He wasn't going to be drawn back into the world of criminality any more than he could help – not now that he'd discovered the joy of going straight; not now that he had Donna.

'I don't want your money,' he said. 'I just want to be left alone.'

Clyde glanced at Bonnie.

'We can do that for you, Kevin,' he said. 'Only not just yet. There's something else we've got in mind: something more... ambitious. And you're not going to let us down, are you?'

# CHAPTER 13

## i

QUENTIN ELDRIDGE-CATTERMOLE stood on the steps of Lyle St Ives gazing down at Porthmeor Beach. The tide was in retreat, leaving a dark band of sand on the edge of which Ezra Cairns could be seen strolling in his distinctive green duffel coat and mustard-yellow cap. How Eldridge-Cattermole despised him, with his outmoded views on art and his pokey gallery selling figurative daubs! No one more thoroughly epitomised the provincialism of this ghastly town: he even talked of 'the St Ives Lyle', as if the whole fashion for inversion had passed him by.

For Eldridge-Cattermole, the directorship here had been both a promotion and a penance. Being part of the Lyle family brought kudos aplenty; but here, three hundred miles from London, he felt like a centurion guarding the furthest reaches of the Roman Empire. He escaped to the capital and international art fairs whenever he could, working the room assiduously at openings and parties; but the travelling was costly, and there was only so much he could claim on expenses. His three years in Cornwall felt like an eternity.

Now, though, that might all be about to change. Marina Bright's words of encouragement rang warmly in his ears.

Humming 'Things Can Only Get Better', he set off for the parking space he had wrested so satisfyingly from Cairns. The Range Rover, looming above the neighbouring cars like Captain Ahab's great white whale, had been almost a financial stretch too far; but his new job – as he already thought of it – would put that worry behind him. And the car, after all, must have helped his status with the trustees. He was off now to collect Koribo, along with his gallerist and social media manager, from St Erth's station. They were bound to be impressed.

The balloon project, Koribo had told him, was progressing rapidly. So excited was the artist by the concept that he had completed the design in a matter of days. The dirigible was now under construction in Germany; the purpose of the artist's visit was to determine which of the sculptures in Barbara Hepworth's garden it should be tethered to.

Eldridge-Cattermole was just wondering what kind of gallerist had a gallery big enough to house giant balloons when a black SUV drew up beside him and two people climbed out.

'Hello, Quentin,' said Clyde.

The hum froze on Eldridge-Cattermole's lips. Suddenly it seemed that things could only get worse.

'What are you doing here?' he asked.

'We came to thank you for recommending young Kevin.

"Who can find us an art forger?" I said to myself. "I know – that bloke Quentin who asked us to fence those Barbara Hepworth maquettes." And how right I was. He's a very talented young man, that Kevin. And he's done a first-rate Van Gogh. I reckon he'll go far.'

'We thought you might like to see it,' said Bonnie.

'No, no,' said Eldridge-Cattermole. 'There's no need for that. I'll take your word for it.'

'It might help you, though.'

'Help me? In what way?'

'We need you to authenticate it,' said Clyde.

Eldridge-Cattermole was aghast.

'Me? But I'm not a Van Gogh expert. It's not my period – not my period at all.'

'The people we're dealing with won't know that. They'll see "Director of Lyle St Ives" and they'll be dead impressed.'

'Even more impressed if they see "Director of Lyle Modern",' said Bonnie. 'As we hear they might.'

'I can't,' said Eldridge-Cattermole desperately. 'My reputation – it's too risky. You'll have to find someone else.'

'Easier said than done,' said Clyde. 'And as you tipped us off about young Kevin, and were well paid for it – as you will be for this little favour – it seems…'

'Appropriate,' said Bonnie.

'Exactly,' said Clyde.

'I can't,' Eldridge-Cattermole repeated. 'It's as simple as that.'

'I don't think so,' said Clyde. 'What if your friend Marina Bright was to find out how exactly those Barbara Hepworth maquettes went missing? I'd say bye bye Lyle Modern.'

'And bye bye Lyle St Ives,' said Bonnie.

'And hello chokey,' said Clyde. 'So I think you'd better say yes.'

Eldridge-Cattermole stared at the shining motor car that had led him so far astray.

'All right,' he said at last. 'On condition that the authentication is never made public.'

'Agreed,' said Clyde.

'And after this you'll leave me alone.'

'Of course.'

Clyde turned to Bonnie and gave her a wink.


ii


'What's next, Natalie?'

'The Unprivileging of Human Intellect Bill, Prime Minister.'

'Right. How did the focus groups go?'

'Better than we could ever have guessed. It's electoral gold dust. A government which was felt to be dragging its feet over instinctivism is now being seen to take the initiative. And Bert as the public face of the campaign is a cast-iron vote-winner.'

Hearing his name, the Jack Russell launched a volley of yaps.

'Has that dog had a walk today?'

'The Health Secretary took him for a run in the park before breakfast, Prime Minister.'

'Tell him to do a few more laps next time. The wretched animal never seems to sleep. My uncle's Labrador slept the whole time. Basket, Bert.'

The dog ignored him.

The Prime Minister sighed. The truth was that Bert was getting on his nerves. Never act with animals or children, went the show-business maxim: how true it was! He couldn't go anywhere without Bert stealing the limelight. He envisaged the dog meeting an unfortunate end just before the next election to bring in the sympathy vote.

'No drawbacks to the Bill, then, Natalie?' he asked.

'None. The fact that an animal will be a legal entity able to, say, sit on the board of a company won't make any difference to anything, because of course that's not going to happen. The Bill will get All God's Creatures onside without costing us anything.'

'Excellent. Add it to the legislation list, will you? We should be able to manage something in six months or so.'

'Of course, Prime Minister.'

Bert finally retired to his basket, and for the next few minutes all Grigoriev could hear at his listening post was a contented snoring.

### iii

'Brilliant, Anton!' said Ogorodnikov. 'Even by your standards it's a stroke of genius.'

'Thank you, your lordship.'

'I'd like those commercial letting calculations as soon as possible – and some ground plans for the building. Put everything else on the back burner.'

Anton set to work; but he could only bring half his mind to the problem. Mathematical formulae no longer interested him in the way writing a novel did – and *A Lot To Look Forward To* was making excellent progress.

Pip had been invited to the house of a rich neighbour called Miss Havisham. She was an eccentric lady, but she was always immaculately turned out in fashionable silks, and her equally immaculate house was full of sunshine and the merry chimes of her clock collection. The only irritation for Pip was a servant girl called Estella who kept following him around and trying to make friends with him. What on earth was he to do about her?

## iv

Ben had never had much luck with relationships. As a teenager he had been hopelessly shy; not until his second year as a theology student had he found a girlfriend. That romance had foundered over her belief in an imminent apocalypse; there followed a series of long, unrequited crushes. A well-meaning friend suggested that he was setting his sights too high by pursuing formidably beautiful and intelligent women – advice he came to resent even more when they settled for dullards or remained forever single. In his late twenties a new pattern emerged, as women doubtful of their long-term boyfriends considered him briefly as an alternative, only to return to their original partners. Ben, hurt and baffled, started to believe that bachelordom was his inescapable fate.

But now there was Anita – and what a remarkable woman she was! So dynamic, so principled, so determined! There was certainly never a dull moment when she was around. He hoped she would approve of his choice of venue for their first official date – the small rear garden of one of the West End's most discreet hotels.

They had barely sat down when the waiter brought them two glasses of champagne.

'With the compliments of the gentleman over there,' he said.

Ben looked up in surprise. Two tables away a tall, very thin young man in a chalk-stripe suit raised his glass. He had an open, smiling face, long black hair and green eyes.

Ben, however, felt more irritated than grateful. What business did this stranger have intruding on such a private occasion?

'Sorry,' he said. 'Do we know each other?'

The young man laughed. 'Not as such. But I couldn't help noticing the two of you looking so happy together, and I thought, "This is something that must be celebrated!" I do hope you don't mind.'

'Of course we don't,' said Anita. 'You're very kind.'

Ben was not so sure. There was something decidedly odd

about this stranger. He couldn't have been more than twenty-five, but behaved as if he were seventy. As for his accent, it was impossible to place, but there was certainly a foreign element to it, begging the question of how he spoke English with such casual grace.

'I do love this place,' said the stranger. 'I would go so far as to say that it's my favourite hideaway in London: far from the world's ignoble strife and all that. What a wonderful phrase! Though I can't for the life of me remember who wrote it. Thomas Hardy?'

'Thomas Gray, actually,' said Ben, 'though Hardy used his phrase "far from the madding crowd" as the title of his novel.'

'Of course! But then, where ignorance is bliss 'tis folly to be wise. Didn't Gray write that as well?'

'He did.'

The stranger laughed again. 'Could we possibly change the subject? I don't want to embarrass myself further in front of a distinguished man of letters like yourself.'

Ben stared at him. 'You know who I am?'

'Of course. I used to read *Cathedral* avidly in my days as a seminarian. Your editorials were the highlight of my week.'

'You mean you're a priest?' said Anita.

'Alas, no. I did attempt the journey, Ms Scott, but the path proved too steep for me, and the barren lands too unforgiving.'

It was Anita's turn to be astonished. 'And how do you know who *I* am?'

'I was present at the General Synod when you made your

dramatic intervention. A splendid piece of theatre, if I may say so – not that I mean to denigrate your stand, which was wholly admirable.'

'I think you'd better tell us *your* name,' said Ben.

'Ivan Dmitry O'Hagan, at your service. And before you ask, yes, I'm half Russian and half Irish. My mother grew up in Moscow, and my father met her when he was posted there as a diplomat.'

'It sounds like an interesting combination,' said Anita.

'You might call it that. He was very Catholic and she was very Orthodox – and as the two churches are traditionally at daggers drawn, it wasn't altogether easy. But they loved each other very much – still do. Of that there is no doubt.'

'So did you grow up in Moscow?'

'Partly. Here, there and everywhere, to be honest. Such is the fate of the diplomatic child.'

'And what are you doing now?'

'To be honest, I'm not quite sure. There are many professions that interest me. And perhaps I don't need to be tied to just one in this day and age. Look at you, Ben – may I call you Ben? One day a magazine editor, the next a cocktail pianist.'

'How the hell do you know about that?'

'I happened to be at Chicane on the memorable night when you came to Anita's rescue. I was one of Oleg Ogorodnikov's party.'

'You're a friend of that bastard?'

'Far from it. My beloved aunt is married to him. Now they're getting divorced, and she's not at all happy with the terms he's offering. I believe that you can help her. She'd like you to come to elevenses.' He stood up and offered Ben a card. 'There are the details. Text me if there's a problem. In the meantime, I wish you joy of the evening.'

Giving a small bow, he turned and stalked away.

# CHAPTER 14

## i

THOUGH WARY OF Ivan O'Hagan's invitation, Ben was attracted by the idea of elevenses. Mid-morning refreshment was a hallmark of British civilisation shamefully neglected in the hurly-burly of twenty-first century life. At school it had been synonymous with a blissful break from lessons; at university, a chance to foster friendships between lectures. And during those happy days at *Cathedral*, his staff had known never to ask for an eleven o'clock meeting: the hour would find him slipping across the road for a cappuccino and an almond croissant with a copy of the *Church Times* or *The Tablet* under his arm. Now, all too often, people spoke of having three meals a day, as if elevenses and afternoon tea were not essential to one's strength and one's sanity.

'I can just imagine what her house is like,' said Anita as their minicab made its way towards Mayfair through streets shiny with rain. 'Over-the-top oligarch bling everywhere. Will you still love me if I throw up?'

Ben had not actually told her that he loved her; even if he had been certain on the point himself, previous disappointments had made him wary of premature declarations. All he could say was that he found it profoundly cheering, after all his trials and tribulations, to have someone so affectionate and vivacious in his life: to wake up each morning to the prospect of seeing her gave him a thrill of a kind he had almost forgotten. Whatever the outcome of their visit to Lady Ogorodnikov, he was happy to think that it would give them one more thing in common.

The house was in a street which, despite its proximity to Piccadilly and Park Lane, was extraordinarily quiet. A butler in a white jacket and white gloves showed them up to a drawing room on the first floor.

Anita's prediction proved entirely wrong. The house was the epitome of good taste: carefully restored cornices; walls painted a delicate duck-egg blue; nineteenth-century French chairs upholstered in fine linen; classical prints of Moscow and St Petersburg; chintz curtains with a subtle tree-of-life motif; a bright Suzani tablecloth. Of sumptuous marble and gilding there was no sign.

Ivan O'Hagan rose to meet them.

'Welcome,' he said. 'How good of you to come.'

'What a beautiful room,' said Anita.

'Thank you. I'm starting to think that interior design might be my way forward. I'm particularly pleased with the tablecloth: 1960s, would you believe? I found it in Uzbekistan.'

'Do you travel a lot?' asked Ben.

'When I can. The diplomatic heritage, I suppose.'

'Have you thought of a diplomatic career?'

'Difficult with my dual nationality, I'm afraid. The Irish would be afraid I was spying for the Russians, and the Russians would be quite certain I was spying for the Irish. But please – have a seat.'

Ben and Anita sank into what felt like several fathoms of spotless cream sofa.

'My aunt will be here any moment,' Ivan O'Hagan went on. 'I must warn you that her English is limited. She understands most things, but lacks confidence in speaking. She learnt a few – how shall I put it? – colloquial phrases when she went to my parents' wedding in Ireland, but never got much beyond that, so forgive me if I do most of the talking. Ah – here she is now.'

Lady Ogorodnikov was a compact woman of indeterminate age. Her hair was very black and her nails were very pink; she wore a beautifully tailored black dress with two strings of pearls and a diamond brooch. Her features had been so enhanced by cosmetic surgery that it was hard to tell what she might originally have looked like. She may have attempted a smile; if so, her facial muscles failed her.

Her accent, unlike her nephew's, left no doubt about her Russian heritage. 'The top of the morning,' she said, with heavy Slavic vowels. 'A hundred thousand welcomes.'

'Thank you,' said Ben.

'It is a soft day altogether.'

'It is indeed.'

'Are you keeping well?'

'Yes, thank you.'

Her stock of pleasantries apparently exhausted, Lady Ogorodnikov sat down and rang a little silver bell.

If her house's décor showed restraint, the menu for elevenses did not. The butler brought a silver coffee pot, a jug of fresh orange juice and a bottle of champagne. He brought croissants, madeleines, profiteroles and éclairs. He brought smoked salmon sandwiches, blinis smothered with sour cream and caviare, and water biscuits topped with pâté de foie gras. Ben regretted having eaten breakfast.

'This is very generous,' he said, surveying the panoply of plates, glasses, coffee cups and luxury foodstuffs. 'May I ask how you think we can help you?'

'As I mentioned,' said Ivan O'Hagan, 'my aunt is in the throes of a divorce. Despite the long years of devoted marital support she's given my uncle, he's decided to cast her aside in favour of a young woman half his age.'

'Fecking floozie,' said Lady Ogorodnikov.

'Naturally,' Ivan O'Hagan went on, 'my aunt is deeply upset by his infidelity and ingratitude. To add insult to injury, Oleg is going to great lengths to conceal his assets so that she doesn't receive a fair settlement.'

'A gombeen man entirely,' said Lady Ogorodnikov.

'Uncle Oleg's business practices are shady to say the least. There's hardly an illicit activity in which he hasn't been involved. No court which knows his true character would give credence to his estimates of his wealth.

'Unfortunately he's a past master of covering his tracks – hence his success in purchasing a peerage. Forensic

accountants who've pursued him have found themselves outsmarted at every turn.'

'The little gobshite,' said Lady Ogorodnikov.

'There is, however, one way in which he might be brought
to book. One of his criminal activities involves faking important works of art. Each is executed to the highest standards,
and supplied with an apparently impeccable provenance. And
he's recently put one up for sale.'

'I read that he's selling a Chagall,' said Anita.

'Supposedly, yes. He claims that it was part of a private
collection seized by the Soviet state in the 1920s. Thanks to
the current obsession with instinctivism, its subject – a flying
cow – makes it of particular interest. It's expected to fetch
twenty million pounds at auction.'

'But that money will be factored into his wealth by the
divorce court,' said Ben. 'So why's he selling it now, rather
than hiding it in a bank vault?'

'That's part of Oleg's cunning. He's making a public pre-
tence of being transparent in order to convince the judge. As
far as he's concerned it's a loss leader: twenty million pounds
is a small price to pay to conceal the true extent of his wealth.'

'The little bollocks,' said Lady Ogorodnikov.

'So what's this got to do with us?' asked Anita.

'Just as Al Capone was brought to book for tax evasion, we
believe that Uncle Oleg can be brought down by the least of
his crimes – art fraud. We'd like Ben to buy the picture with
money which my aunt will supply; once it's in our hands, we
can prove that it's a fake, and that Uncle Oleg was aware of
it all along. His credibility will be destroyed. With luck he'll

go to prison.'

'But why me?' asked Ben.

'Because you are a perfect English gentleman unknown to Uncle Oleg and a newcomer to the art market: the last person, in his eyes, who would suspect a fake. And because we believe that you and Anita are as keen to bring him down as we are.'

'But he does know me. He's seen me playing the piano at Chicane.'

'Rest assured that Uncle Oleg doesn't notice little people – and I'm afraid that as far as he's concerned, that's what you are.'

'What about the auction house? Won't they think it odd that my first venture into the art market is to spend twenty million on a Chagall?'

'It's not in their interest to ask questions like that. All they'll want to know is that you can come up with the cash. We can ensure that's not a problem.'

'Why not just bid anonymously yourselves?'

'Because anonymity can't ultimately be guaranteed. It would be too big a risk.'

'And what about proving it's a fake?' asked Anita. 'How can you be sure of doing that?'

'When you're unsure that something is a fake, it's difficult. But when you *know* that it's a fake, you know what to look for. As for the provenance, that's been cooked up by an assistant of Uncle Oleg's called Anton Ivanovich. We believe that we can persuade him to spill the beans. What do you say?'

'I'll think about it,' said Ben.

'He'll do it,' said Anita.

'Great man yourself,' said Lady Ogorodnikov.

ii

So Ben and Anita had their first quarrel.

'What do you mean,' he demanded, 'dropping me in it like that? I said I needed to think about it, and I do. We hardly know these people: we've met her once and him twice. I have no idea whether they're trustworthy.'

'Something has to be done to stop Ogorodnikov. If he's allowed to demolish those churches, it'll be your fault: you should never have given All God's Creatures the time of day. Now we've been handed a chance to foil him on a plate. We can't afford to pass it up.'

'How do we know he hasn't put them up to it? It could be a trap.'

'Why would he bother? As we know, he doesn't notice little people.'

'We only have Ivan's word for that. Anyway, I'm not a little person. I've edited a highly respected magazine and commissioned some of the finest writers in the land.'

'That was before you became a cocktail pianist.'

'Which meant that I just I happened to be there when you needed someone to save your skin.'

They looked at each other and burst out laughing.

'All right,' said Anita. 'I'm sorry: I just got carried away when they made that suggestion. If you're worried about it, why don't you ask for a trial run – get them to let you bid a couple of million for something else? Then we'll see whether they're serious. I'm sure they can spare the money.'

Ben kissed her.

'OK,' he said. 'I will.'

### iii

Jennifer Pettifer was thrilled to be put in charge of the council's instinctivism audit. At last her mastery of regulation and small print was receiving the recognition it deserved: this, surely, was her chance to earn a lasting place in the annals of local bureaucracy.

At moments, however, the scale of the task overwhelmed her. Where to begin? The libraries seemed the easiest answer: all those shelves stuffed with volumes honouring an outdated creed. *Animal Farm*, with its profound disrespect for pigs, clearly had to go, as did *Ferdinand the Bull* with its faux sympathy for cattle. *Watership Down*, that shameless appropriation of rabbits' stories, was another prime candidate. But they were just the tip of the iceberg: she would need a dedicated team to check all the other suspect titles. Thank goodness Pamela had passed on *Cathedral*'s carefully compiled list of proscribed authors – that would at least buy some time.

Then there was the lack of recognition for other creatures in public places. For a county called Oxfordshire, it was nothing short of a scandal. She envisaged an adjunct to the Martyrs' Memorial celebrating admirable animals. The university must play its part: perhaps the colleges could be pressured into re-wilding their quadrangles as habitats for field mice and other small rodents. Worcester College, of course, had a lake: she wondered idly if it might accommodate some water buffalo.

She felt privileged – if she dared use that word – to be part of the movement her niece now headed. Rules had been meat and drink to her ever since she joined the civil service, and now she could make them up as she went along: should anyone presume to challenge her, she had only to whisper 'Anti-instinctivist!' and they would shrink from her sight.

Yes, she had much to be thankful to Pamela for. And here was an email from her now, labelled 'Highly confidential'. Intrigued, Jennifer clicked on it.

*Dear Auntie Jennifer,* it read.

*We're just doing some blue-sky thinking on this at the moment, and would really welcome your input as someone who knows her way around the planning laws.*

*Best love,*

*Pamela*

Jennifer opened the attachment and there it was:

ST PAUL'S CATHEDRAL, REPURPOSING OF WORSHIP SPACE: VETERINARIAN HOSPITAL AND LUXURY APARTMENTS.

Ben's first foray into the art market went remarkably smoothly. Lady Ogorodnikov happened to have her eye on a Lucien Freud being auctioned the following week. It was a portrait, little bigger than a postcard, of a society beauty whom the Master had laboured to make ferociously ugly: gazing at the perfect brush strokes which had given her the pallor of a dead fish, Ben could think of nothing he would less like to have on his wall. But it had a guide price of two and a half to three million pounds, and Lady Ogorodnikov had indicated a willingness to pay two million more; and so Ben, with the glee inherent in spending someone else's money, found himself giving nods worth hundreds of thousands from the back of the saleroom.

After a flurry of early bids, the guide price had easily been reached. Now only two people remained in the contest: Ben and an elderly lady whose Bohemian appearance suggested that she might have been one of Freud's mistresses in her youth.

'Three million five hundred thousand,' said the auctioneer. 'Against you, sir. Do I hear three point six?'

How thrilling it was! To be standing here, bidding more money than he had earned in his life, with the eyes of inquisitive connoisseurs and pretty sale-room assistants fixed upon him! For a moment he felt a strange kinship with the oligarch whose ruthless pursuit of wealth had brought about this gratifying situation. Might he, Ben Fairweather, have been equally acquisitive if he had been born in a decaying Moscow tower block instead of a comfortable Victorian villa?

At last the elderly lady shook her head.

'Gone to the gentleman at the back for five million pounds!' proclaimed the auctioneer. A ripple of applause ran through the room.

Afterwards Ben was fêted as never before. No work of art, it transpired, had sold for so much per square inch. Everyone at the sale seemed keen to make his acquaintance, either to cultivate him as a future client or size him up as a rival collector. Invitations to lunch – to a glass or two of champagne – to view a very unusual and special work – fluttered down on him like cherry blossom in May. Nobody, to his relief, recognised him as the journalist who had earned the hatred of every right-minded liberal in the land. The chairman of the auction house had just promised to email him when Ivan O'Hagan glided through the crowd as if on an invisible skateboard.

'Well done, Ben,' he said. 'I've just been on the phone to my aunt and she's delighted. I hope you're feeling reassured about our arrangement.'

Looking Ivan full in the face, Ben decided that he liked him after all.

v

'I'm sorry,' said the Prime Minister, 'I don't see the problem. Yes, I gave a speech at the Cambridge Union when I was nineteen: rather a good one, as I remember. Yes, I said that democracy didn't have a cat's chance in hell of surviving in Russia. Events proved me right. So what's this news agency so excited about?'

Natalie and the press secretary exchanged a glance.

'It was your choice of words, Prime Minister,' said Natalie. 'A cat's chance in hell.'

'Enlighten me.'

'Cats don't go to hell. Like all animals, they go straight to heaven. At least, that's All God's Creatures' position.'

'Nonsense! What about all those witches' familiars? They can hardly have been a shoo-in for celestial bliss.'

'That's old superstition, not progressive theology. Unless we nip this in the bud, it could seriously damage you at the polls.'

'But it was a figure of speech. And I was nineteen!'

'That's irrelevant, I'm afraid. Your critics will paint you as a lifelong, dyed-in-the-wool anti-instinctivist.'

'Are we still allowed to dye wool? Are you sure that isn't breaching sheep's rights?'

'Please, Prime Minister.'

The Prime Minister drummed his fingers on the desk and stared at the photograph beside him. It showed him in his first term of office, before his hair began to go grey, addressing the US Senate with all the confidence of a vote-winning matinée idol. How had he become the plaything of theological fads and fanatics?

'All right, Natalie. What do you suggest?'

'Have Bert received into the Church of England as soon as possible. That will get you headlines everywhere, and crowd these accusations out of the news.'

'And what does that involve? Do I need to book Westminster Abbey and round up some heads of state as godparents? Will the Archbishop of Canterbury officiate?'

'*Please*, Prime Minister.'

'All right, go on.'

'The archbishop, as you know, is very anti All God's Creatures. The most senior churchman sympathetic to their cause is the Bishop of Durham. I understand that she's carried out several such ceremonies. All it involves is a laying on of hands.'

The Prime Minister nodded wearily.

'All right,' he said. 'Sound her out. And maybe we could commission some souvenir mugs and tea towels to mark the occasion. The Exchequer's coffers are a little low at the moment.'

Shifting in his basket, Bert gave a small snuffle of approval.

# CHAPTER 15

i

THE CHAGALL – OR PSEUDO-CHAGALL – was certainly a striking piece of work. The cow at its centre was a magnificent, charming beast, showing a suggestion of a smile as – horns garlanded with flowers – it flew over the onion domes of a Russian town. A colourful crowd stared up at it, while a pair of rosy-cheeked angels guided it on its way. A golden sun cast its beneficent rays from the top right-hand corner.

'A masterpiece, without question,' said the chairman of the auction house, wiping his mouth with an eau-de-nil silk handkerchief.

'Absolutely,' said Ben.

After his initial hesitancy, he had come to feel more than comfortable in his role as an affluent collector. This private viewing in the boardroom, with a waitress standing by to refill his glass of champagne and proffer exquisite canapés, seemed no more than his due.

He examined the painting more closely. Somewhere under his nose was a clue to its recent execution, but he was damned if he could tell what it was. A pigment that wasn't quite right? A hesitant brushstroke? A misreading of bovine anatomy? Ivan O'Hagan and his experts would have to pinpoint the chink in Ogorodnikov's armour, because spotting it was certainly beyond him.

'One can't overestimate the work's importance,' said the chairman. 'It predates his *Cow with a Parasol* by at least twenty years. And being so overtly religious, so in tune with the current zeitgeist – I think one could confidently call it an icon for our times.'

'Prophetic, you might say.'

'Prophetic indeed.'

'And you mentioned you'd had a lot of interest?'

'Oh, yes: from the States, Japan, China. But of course we'd like to sell to a British buyer.'

Ben imagined the painting hanging in the National Gallery. 'On loan from the Ben Fairweather Collection', the label would read. He wondered what kind of frame would show it to its best advantage. What a shame that it was a fake, and that he was not buying it for himself.

If Ivan Dmitry O'Hagan had a fault, it was overconfidence. Had Ben been aware of this, he might have been less carried away by their joint enterprise.

Yes, the Chagall was a fake, and the experts Ivan had on hand were well qualified to prove it. But establishing that Uncle Oleg *knew* it to be a fake was another matter, and could only be achieved with Anton Ivanovich's co-operation.

Ivan's reasoning was as follows. It was unlikely that Anton could be bought, given the rewards that his employer was able to heap upon him. That left blackmail. He must have something to hide, because everybody did – particularly those associated with Uncle Oleg. And there must be a clue to it somewhere on the internet, because there always was.

Ivan poured himself a glass of wine and began his search.

First up was Anton's CV. Born in Moscow, he had studied computer sciences at the city's Technological University, done national service in the Russian army, reaching the rank of second lieutenant, then qualified as an accountant. Over the past two years he had worked in that capacity for several companies in the Ogorodnikov empire. So far, so boring.

But his social media posts told a different story. Here he was at Glastonbury, rolling in the mud like a creature born of the primordial slime. A month later he could be found at a stag party in Bratislava, doing shots while a Slovakian strongman held him upside down by his ankles. Then it was off to Ibiza, where sunset found him at a beachside bar with a bikini-clad girl on each arm – not the pale figure Ivan had seen on video calls, but a bronzed young Adonis.

And what was that on the bottle-strewn table in front of him? Ivan's sharp eyes were quick to identify it: a tiny plastic packet of white powder. Cocaine! Now he was getting somewhere.

### iii

'Beep! Beep!' went the alarm system.

Really, thought Anton, it was too annoying. Here he was in the middle of a moving farewell scene – Pip saying goodbye to his beloved sister as he set sail to seek his fortune in Australia – and some bastard had to pick this moment to try to hack his emails.

Who on earth could it be?

### iv

The sun was shining on Durham Cathedral as the Prime Minister's cavalcade came to a halt in front of the great north door. The gold thread on the bishop's mitre sparkled as she waited to greet him; she had, however, dispensed with her crook, now widely recognised as a symbol of ovine repression. Outside-broadcast vehicles were parked nose-to-tail around Palace Green; a large crowd of well-wishers were camped out on the grass, waiting to watch the ceremony on a giant screen. The small contingent of Young Humanist protestors had been bundled into police vans and detained under the Prevention of Terrorism Act.

'A lovely day for it,' said the bishop, shaking the Prime Minister's hand. 'And this is Bert, if I'm not mistaken.'

'Indeed it is. A handsome little fellow, don't you think?'

Bert wagged his tail and sniffed at the hem of the bishop's robes.

'Very. And that's a very smart collar he's wearing. I wonder if you might remove it before the ceremony, though: I think he should be received into the Church in his natural state.'

Although the word 'godparents' did not appear on the service sheet, three sponsors had been found for the occasion: the chair of the RSPCA, the secretary of the Kennel Club and Pamela Pettifer. Watching at home, her aunt Jennifer felt a bittersweet pang of pride and jealousy. Of course she loved Pammy; of course she was glad that her niece had escaped academic obscurity; but that the Prime Minister should be laying his hand helpfully on the small of her back, not Jennifer's – it was just too unfair!

The organ swelled and the choristers gave their all to the opening hymn, 'All Creatures That on Earth Do Dwell'. The dean, conscious of the television scheduling, rattled through the opening prayers. Then the bishop took to the pulpit.

She had chosen as her text the story of Jonah and the whale, and the Old Testament prophet's mantle seemed to descend on her as she hit her stride.

'Repent, ye bipeds!' she cried. 'Repent, ye who have

presumed to raise mankind above the beasts of the field, the fish of the sea and the fowls of the air!'

The Prime Minister glanced at Natalie and rolled his eyes. Bert fidgeted in his lap.

'Jonah defied the word of God,' the bishop continued. 'Rather than preach to the hostile people of Nineveh, he tried to flee across the sea. But when the sailors threw him overboard, the "great fish" – the whale – obeyed his Maker's command and swallowed the prophet up. What clearer example could there be of man's inferior role in creation?'

On and on she ranted. The television schedulers watched their monitors anxiously. An elderly man who rose to his feet with a shout of 'Heresy!' was hustled away. Bert dozed. The Prime Minister wondered why he hadn't heard from Oleg Ogorodnikov that week, and what Pamela Pettifer would be like in bed. At last the sermon came to an end.

'Who doth this dog bring as his companions in churching?' demanded the bishop.

The Prime Minister stepped forward. Pamela, the chair of the RSPCA and the secretary of the Kennel Club followed.

Bert, never at his most amenable when suddenly awoken, wriggled petulantly in the Prime Minister's arms. It was then that he caught sight of the cathedral cat.

Abednego – a surly, spiteful tortoiseshell – had once been persona non grata in the cathedral precincts, cursed and shooed away by clergy and choristers alike. But the rise of All God's Creatures had transformed his fortunes. Organic scraps from the Undercroft Café and titbits from the bishop's kitchen were his for the asking.

In Bert, however, he discerned a rival for this tithe. Consequently, he gave his most aggressive hiss.

Bert knew a challenge when he heard one. Oblivious to the bishop's welcoming words, he made a bid for freedom; but the Prime Minister's grip was firm. Frustrated, Bert sank his teeth into his owner's index finger.

What followed would be shared many thousands of times on social media. With a cry of pain, the Prime Minister let go; Bert fell towards the floor. But before he hit it, the Prime Minister's foot – imbued with a muscle memory of youthful days on the football field – shot forward and made full contact with the terrier's ribs. Bert sailed through the air and landed at the base of a massive pillar.

The congregation stared aghast.

Bert lay stunned – but only for a moment. His focus was not on his human antagonist but his feline one. Seeing Abednego vanishing in the direction of the south transept, he started after him with a furious bark, and seconds later was gone from sight.

v

'You've got her now,' said the Archbishop's wife delightedly as the head of the Church of England rose to turn off the television. 'A bishop allowing an act of brutality like that in her own cathedral! Whatever happened to safeguarding? You must demand her resignation immediately. None of those ghastly instinctivists will stand by her.'

'Well, well,' said the Archbishop. 'It may not be an original observation, but...God moves in a mysterious way.'

## vi

'How bad is it?' asked the Prime Minister. He was back at his Downing Street office, where Bert's empty basket was a constant reminder of the morning's fiasco.

'As bad as it could be,' said Natalie. 'Everyone from the Leader of the Opposition to the Poet Laureate is calling for your resignation. Twenty of your own backbenchers say they would support a vote of no confidence. There's a strong chance of a leadership challenge.'

'Any way out?'

'We've tried the "moment of madness" line, but it isn't gaining any traction. Now we're briefing that you were trying to break Bert's fall with your foot but were caught off balance. The RSPCA guy has agreed to go along with that in return for a knighthood, as has the Kennel Club man. We're hoping Pamela Pettifer might accept a chair at Oxford or Cambridge.'

'But you're not sure it will do the trick?'

'To be honest, no – particularly with Bert still missing. There's really only one card you can play at this point.'

'And what's that?'

'The Unprivileging of Human Intellect Bill. Move it to the top of the parliamentary agenda. Tell the nation it's an act of atonement. That might just do the trick.'

The Prime Minister thought of the men and women who had sat within these four walls before him. He had hoped to be remembered for great infrastructure projects and international trade agreements. Now they must take second place because he'd kicked a stupid mutt. He thought of Harold Macmillan's wise words on the ultimate pitfall of politics: 'Events, dear boy, events.'

'Very well,' he sighed. 'Do it.'

# CHAPTER 16

## i

'COME IN, FATHER PETER,' said Mrs Petrovna. 'How good of you to spare the time to come here. Let me introduce you to my lodger, Ben Fairweather.'

Father Peter was not at all as Ben had imagined. In his mind's eye, he had pictured the guest at Mrs Petrovna's tea party as a pale, nervous young curate getting used to his first beardy. Instead, a muscular middle-aged man with a broken nose dominated the drawing room.

'Why don't you make yourself comfortable on the sofa, Father?' said Mrs Petrovna. 'Ben, you take the armchair. I'll just go and put the kettle on.'

The two men settled themselves on the chintz cushions.

'I gather you're a newcomer to London, Father,' said Ben.

'Yes.' There was a pause. 'Excuse me, my English is not very good.'

'Better than my Russian, I'm sure. But I do know the word

for trolleybus.'

Father Peter looked blank.

'Because, of course, it's the same as in English: *trolleybus*,' Ben explained with a smile.

His joke made no impression.

Ben tried again. 'How are you finding our country?'

'It is very beautiful. I like your Hyde Park.'

'I'm sure Moscow has beautiful parks as well.'

'Not so many.'

'Do you come from Moscow?'

'No. From a little town you will not have heard of.'

'Ah.'

Ben wished that Mrs Petrovna would hurry up with the tea.

'You must be very busy at the cathedral,' he said.

'Yes.' Father Peter fingered the cross hanging from his neck.

'I've been there a couple of times. It's a fine building.'

'Yes.' Father Peter stared at the cross as if he had never seen one before.

'Do you have a large team of clergy?'

Father Peter hesitated.

'No.' He let the cross settle again on his broad chest.

Ben cast around desperately for another topic of conversation. Glancing up, he caught sight of the icons on top of Mrs Petrovna's bookcase.

'I had a very interesting chat recently with an art dealer,' he said. 'He'd discovered a portrait of the Virgin and Child which he believed dated from before the iconoclasm.'

'The iconoclasm?'

'You know, the period in the eighth century when the Emperor Constantine banned religious pictures and most of them were destroyed.'

Father Peter looked mystified.

'It is a subject of particular interest to the Metropolitan,' he said at last. 'You should ask him about it.'

At last Mrs Petrovna returned with a tray. There were cucumber sandwiches, gingernut biscuits and a spectacularly sticky cake from a smart patisserie.

'Sorry to interrupt,' she said. 'The two of you must have so much to talk about.'

From then on, to Ben's relief, it was she who did most of the talking. The Metropolitan's health, the cathedral's state of repair, her favourite saints – all these subjects fuelled her animated chatter.

Though Father Peter remained taciturn, the little he did say made Ben feel that he was like no other priest he had met. In fact he began to wonder if Father Peter really was a priest at all.

Something else disturbed him: the smell of incense.

There should have been no surprise about it: it was a scent bound to impregnate any Orthodox clergyman's clothes. But Ben couldn't stop thinking about the church where Cecil Simpson had met his end.

At last Father Peter got to his feet and said that it was time for him to leave. He thanked Mrs Petrovna, and even stretched to a compliment about the sticky cake.

'Not at all, Father,' said Mrs Petrovna. 'You must come

again.'

On an impulse, Ben darted into his bedroom. He caught up with Father Peter as he made his way along the hall.

'Father! You dropped your handkerchief.'

Father Peter glanced at the crumpled ball of white cotton. 'Thank you,' he said, taking it and putting it in his pocket. Then he headed down the stairs.

## ii

'You did *what*?' said Anita.

'It was just a spur-of-the-moment thing,' said Ben. 'There was this dodgy priest smelling of incense, and this dodgy handkerchief smelling of the same thing. I simply put two and two together. He didn't think twice about taking it.'

'You twerp! You complete and utter idiot! You've given away the only thing linking the murderer to the crime scene. Think how much DNA there must have been on it!'

'But if I've established a link…'

'You haven't established a link! It probably didn't belong to him at all. He only thought it might because you told him he'd dropped it. The chances of a priest having an Olympic hanky seem pretty much nil to me.'

'But if he's not a real priest…'

'Even then it's incredibly far-fetched. Why would a Russian disguise himself as a priest in order to murder an elderly English clergyman?

'And just suppose you're right. Suppose he puts his hand in his pocket and finds he's got another handkerchief in it. Then he realises that he didn't drop the one you handed him, and you're on to him. So what's he going to do? Come back to shut you up, that's what. So you'd better hope that you're wrong. Just don't expect me to hang around and become a known associate.'

She rang off.

Ben sighed. So much for new romance: it was over before it had begun. And the worst of it was that Anita was right: he'd acted like a fool.

Another thing preyed on his mind as he trudged towards Chicane for his evening's work. Should he tell Mrs Petrovna of his suspicions? He didn't like the idea of her being left alone, even when helping out at the cathedral, with a man who, for all Ben knew, might murder elderly people for kicks. On the other hand, Father Peter might be genuine, and the place was so much a part of her life: he didn't want to upset her by casting a shadow over it.

Better, he decided, to keep a close eye on the situation – for her sake, and his.

### iii

It could not be said of Bert that he was enjoying life away from Downing Street. Though he had finally cornered Abednego, he had come off the worse in their encounter and had a ragged ear to show for it. Then there had been an unfortunate meeting with a road-mending team in which the spots on his coat had been augmented by a spattering of tar. He was unrecognisable as the well-groomed animal who had graced the nation's front pages.

He was also very hungry, and as the pangs increased, his fighting spirit deserted him. Traffic, from which he had always been cocooned in luxuriously upholstered limousines, overwhelmed his senses and reduced him to a forlorn, shivering creature. His anxiety to escape the vehicles and their fumes drove him away from the centre of Durham and towards the open spaces on the edges of the city.

It was here that he found a strange sight: an enormous tent with bold stripes in gay colours, flanked by neat rows of cars, trucks and caravans.

Sitting outside the nearest tent was a young woman. She wore a short brown woollen dress with large white polka dots; on her head was a conical orange hat. Her face was extremely white and her nose extremely red. Most interestingly of all, she was eating her lunch.

'Hello, Piccolino,' she said. 'Would you like some of my sandwich?'

iv

Carlotta the Sad Clown had not always been sad. She came, in fact, from a long line of happy clowns, who made the best of

the mixed cards dealt to them by fate, plying their trade sometimes in Britain and sometimes in their native Italy. Carlotta's
parents had given her as good an education as their peripa-
tetic existence allowed, and imbued her with their Catholic
faith as a bulwark against its uncertainties. An apt pupil, she
had occasioned delight and astonishment by becoming the
first member of Bennett's Circus to go to university.

She was quick to make her mark at Exeter, impressing
her fellow students with her beauty, her outgoing personality
and – when cajoled at parties – her slapstick acrobatic skills.
But in her second year she discovered the writings of Albert
Camus and Samuel Beckett. Together they dragged her down
into the slough of despond; she dropped out of university,
and shocked her family by returning to Bennett's not as a
happy clown but as a melancholy one. What could she do in
the face of a hostile, implacable universe, she reasoned, but
cavort in whiteface and absurd costumes, expressing through
mime the hopelessness of the human condition? Her act was
unquestionably brilliant; but when the Big Top fell silent and
the performers wiped away their greasepaint, there were few
who sought her company.

'Poor child – too clever for her own good,' opined Madame
Fleur, the mind-reader. 'What's the point of all that studying
if it only makes you mope from morning till night?'

Today, as fate would have it, Carlotta was reading an old
copy of *Cathedral* as she ate her simple lunch: the very issue
in which Ben had lamented the death of his beloved dog. 'Oh
good-hearted but deluded man!' she thought. Of course there
would be no reunion with the animal after death: annihilation

was all the two would share – the fate of everything that lived under the dying sun.

But here, suddenly, in front of her was another dog. It was a collarless stray, looking much the worse for wear, yet something about its eager face touched her as nothing had done since her student days. She smiled and tore off a corner of cheese and pickle sandwich.

v

Ben's late hours at Chicane meant that he was seldom up in time to breakfast with Mrs Petrovna; but on the day of the auction he rose early, springing from bed with alacrity. He found her reading the newspaper over a cup of coffee and a bowl of cream-infused porridge.

'Good morning, dear,' she said. 'You can help me with the crossword. "Paling undead killer investor": ten letters, first letter S, fifth letter E.'

'Stakeholder,' said Ben. How easily it had come to him! Things today were surely going to go his way.

'Fits perfectly: clever you! Now, I hope you won't say no to bacon and eggs – lovely fresh eggs from my cousin in Sussex.'

As she busied herself in the kitchen, Ben felt his suspicions about her priestly visitor getting the better of him.

'Your friend Father Peter,' he said as he sliced a smoked Danish rasher. 'There were some aspects of Orthodoxy he didn't seem too sure about. But he's not a novice, is he? He's much too old for that.'

Mrs Petrovna smiled. 'You know, my dear, I wonder if your years on that magazine haven't left you a little too focused on the intellectual side of religion. In Russia the tradition of the holy fool is still strong. Father Peter may not be the cleverest of clergymen, but you should see his smile when he swings the censer. Beatific – that's the only word for it: positively beatific. Now, what's "Meditative state conscious of half a monster," eleven letters beginning with M and ending in S? No, don't tell me – mindfulness!'

There was no point, Ben decided, in trying to explain the dark implications of Father Peter's censer-swinging. Today he had other fish to fry.

The saleroom was already crowded when he arrived. Though a seat had been reserved for him, he preferred to take up position by a pillar at the side of the room: it felt somehow more romantic to be a half-hidden participant in the drama that was about to unfold. He looked around for Ivan O'Hagan, but saw no sign of him. Still, there were a hundred lots to be sold before the Chagall.

He felt unexpectedly calm as the moment to start bidding approached. So sure was he of winning that the preliminaries seemed a charade. It was simply a question of how big a bill Lady Ogorodnikov would pick up.

'Lot number 114,' said the auctioneer. '*Cow Ascension* by Marc Chagall.'

They were off!

There was more competition than Ben had expected: no fewer than eight bidders in the lower millions. But one by one they fell away, until only he and an anonymous telephone bidder were left to slug it out.

'Twenty-one million pounds against you, sir,' said the auctioneer. 'Do I hear twenty-one and a half?'

Ben tapped the side of his nose in what he hoped was a nonchalant manner.

'Thank you, sir,' said the auctioneer. 'Twenty-one and a half million pounds I am bid. Do I hear twenty-two?'

All eyes turned to the young woman holding the telephone. She listened for what seemed like a lifetime. But at last she shook her head.

'Any advance on twenty-one and half million pounds?' demanded the auctioneer. 'No? Going once – going twice – sold!'

He brought down his hammer; applause echoed through the room. As Ben was ushered into the leather-panelled VIP lounge, he felt as if he were being carried shoulder high. No matter that the painting was a fake – his credentials as a player in the international art market had been well and truly established.

What followed was a blur. There was champagne; there was more champagne. Executives with increasingly preposterous titles came to congratulate him: there were presidents, vice-presidents and chief officers galore. Some claimed London as their fiefdom; some Europe; some the world. All deferred to him as an A-list client, and looked forward to doing more business with him.

Then there were the journalists, hardly able to believe their luck that the successful bidder for the Chagall had turned up in person, with no apparent desire for anonymity. Yes, art had always been his passion, but it was only now, thanks to an unexpected legacy, that he was able to indulge it. Might he make the painting a gift to the nation, given its instinctivist subject matter? Perhaps. Did he have any thoughts on the disappearance on the Prime Minister's dog? No.

Everything had gone according to plan. Ivan would be delighted. But where *was* Ivan?

Ben reached for his phone, and suddenly remembered: he had put it in airplane mode to avoid being disturbed during the auction. Ivan must have been ringing with congratulations in vain.

He reactivated the device – and there were six missed calls from Ivan, plus a voicemail message, left just as the auction began:

'Ben, I'm afraid we have a problem: my aunt's assets have been frozen. So for God's sake don't bid for the painting – the money isn't there.'

# CHAPTER 17

i

'BANKRUPTCY ISN'T THE END of the world,' said Hughie. 'I've been through it twice. No one thinks the worse of you for it these days: if debtors' prisons still existed, you'd find yourself in pretty good company. I rather wish there was an equivalent for affairs of the heart – you could say to any woman who feels hard done by, "Actually, they're letting me start again with a clean slate."'

Ben couldn't quite see it that way. Fairweathers considered it a point of honour to pay their debts; he would rather go hungry than disgrace the family name. But saving on sandwiches was hardly going to clear the twenty-two million pounds he owed.

'Couldn't you have a word with Lord Ogorodnikov?' he asked Svetlana. 'He obviously thinks you're wonderful.'

She shook her head. 'I would if I could, Ben. But it's strictly a business relationship, and I have to keep it that way.

If anything were to annoy him – well, it could be Chicane looking at bankruptcy.'

'There's no way out,' thought Ben. The auctioneers, once so friendly, were treating him like a pariah. An executive vice-president (European sales and marketing) had made it clear that even if Ogorodnikov agreed to keep the painting, they would still demand their commission. That alone would swallow every penny he owned: he'd have to sell his house and his shares in *Cathedral*. And all because of a painting he knew to be worthless.

Ivan O'Hagan had been apologetic, but claimed there was nothing he could do. Ben, he insisted, should never have turned his phone off, particularly when Ivan failed to appear at the auction.

'Was the whole thing a stitch-up?' Ben wondered. Had the woman he met, with her weird cornucopia of Irish swear words, really been Lady Ogorodnikov? Did the oligarch, far from not noticing little people like nightclub pianists, enjoy grinding them under his heel? 'Never give a sucker an even break,' the saying went – and he, Ben, was surely the biggest sucker of all.

ii

Oleg Ogorodnikov had had another call from the Party Chairman.

'You look very anxious, my tiger,' said Svetlana. 'What is

it?'

'Nothing you need worry about,' said the oligarch, forcing a smile. 'Excuse me a moment.'

He hurried into his office and tapped at his computer. Anton Ivanovich's face appeared on the screen.

'What can I do for you, Lord Ogorodnikov?'

'The Party Chairman wants things speeded up. That fifteen billion is burning a hole in his pocket.'

'This is a highly complicated operation. Everything's going smoothly and fulfilling the criteria I was given. Tell him it is what it is.'

'That's more than my life's worth. Any short cuts you see, take them.'

Anton returned to *A Lot To Look Forward To*, which was reaching an exciting climax. In Australia Pip was about to meet and shoot dead the convict who had threatened him long ago. Then he would return to England and marry Miss Havisham. Learning to write a novel hadn't been easy, but Anton was confident he had cracked it.

'There's no limit to what I can do,' he told himself triumphantly. 'I will conquer the world!'

### iii

'He'll be fine,' said the vet, returning Bert to Carlotta's arms. 'A bit of bruising to the ribs, but nothing to worry about. I'm afraid whoever owned him was a brute. But they didn't get round to microchipping him, so there's no way of identifying him. He'll be far better off with you. I know all you at Bennett's treat your animals well: I look forward to seeing him in action when you've trained him. When will you be back here?'

'We're heading south now, so not until next summer. Perhaps we'll see you then.'

Carlotta had not been planning to train Bert. Though she had worked with dogs in her happy-clown days, it had never occurred to her to include one in her new routine. But now that Bert – or rather, Piccolino, that name having stuck – was a permanent fixture in her life, she began to consider his potential. He was so bright, so affectionate, so eager to learn! Surely there was something they could do together.

Bert, for his part, had found love. Though some people at 10 Downing Street had made a show of petting him, those delegated to walk and feed him had done so grudgingly. The man beside whose desk he had lain had never pretended to like him; nipping his finger in the cathedral was the most satisfying thing Bert had ever done.

But Carlotta! (He had already learned her name.) She kissed and cuddled him at every opportunity; she rubbed his stomach on demand; she played with him; she gave him treats. She was the owner any dog might dream of. He even liked being called Piccolino – those south European syllables sounded so much more musical than 'Bert'. And the multifarious smells of the circus! Yes, this was the life for him.

So depressed was Ben by the prospect of financial ruin that when the coroner's report on the death of Rupert Norris appeared a fortnight later, he could hardly bring himself to read it. But in the end curiosity got the better of him.

There was nothing new in the details the report laid out: the unfortunate man's departure from the Embroiderers' Hall; his fall from the bridge, witnessed only from below; the retrieval of his body, which sometimes came back to Ben in nightmares. Whether foul play had been involved was impossible to determine. An open verdict was recorded.

But the profile of the dead man was another matter. None of those called upon to give evidence considered him suicidal. He had been the life and soul of the guild hall dinner; an enthusiastic member of his local community; a loving and beloved husband and father; a well-respected – and rewarded – banker. He had given generously of his time and expertise, too, as a trustee of Sir John Soane's Museum and a Church Commissioner.

Ben reached for his phone.

'Anita? Are you still talking to me?'

'I suppose so. You may be an idiot, but at least you're a lovable one.'

Ben felt a surge of relief. His mind, however, was on other matters. 'Your friend Cecil Simpson – he wasn't by any chance a Church Commissioner, was he?'

'Since you ask, yes.'

'Then I think we might be on to something.'

# CHAPTER 18

i

'SORRY IT'S TAKEN ME SO LONG,' said Anita when she rang Ben back a few hours later. 'The Church of England's in such a tizz over the split in the synod that my contacts were hard to get hold of. But your hunch was right: Rupert Norris and Cecil Simpson were allies against All God's Creatures and the repurposing of traditional church buildings. There was someone else they were in cahoots with as well: a retired lawyer called Clare Longridge. And guess what? She died not long before Norris in a hit-and-run accident. Only something tells me it wasn't an accident.

'So three people who stood in the way of All God's Creatures have died in mysterious circumstances. Their deaths cleared the way for replacements who would support the demolition of the Wren churches, and the sites' redevelopment by Ogorodnikov.'

Ben whistled. 'Then you think Ogorodnikov had them

killed?'

'It's more than possible.'

'We'd better talk to Inspector Aziz. I'll call him.'

Aziz too was elusive. 'He's up to his eyes for the next couple of days,' Ben finally reported. 'But he says he can meet us at Westminster Pier at two o'clock on Thursday. Are you free?'

'Absolutely.'

'See you then.'

## ii

Kevin was finding it hard to get a grip as he walked towards Donna's flat. Twenty-two million quid for a picture he'd painted! Part of him couldn't help feeling proud; but at the same time…well, he was bound to be found out, wasn't he? The only reason he hadn't been rumbled yet was that everyone *wanted* the painting to be real. The saleroom wanted to make a lot of money, and the media wanted the headline story of a newly discovered instinctivist icon. But once things cooled down, once more clear-eyed experts had had a chance to look at it, the game would surely be up. The police would catch Bonnie and Clyde, who would finger him, and then it would be prison for all of them – maybe the same prison as Big Mario. It didn't bear thinking about.

But he mustn't tell Donna – he was sure of that. The precious thing between them might be doomed, but he would keep it going as long as possible and treasure every minute of it.

'Hello, love,' she said with the brightest of smiles as she opened the front door.

'Hi.'

He took her in his arms; but as he did so, his hug became a convulsion and tears started to his eyes.

'Kev, darling,' she exclaimed. 'What is it?'

And so it all came out.

'There it is,' he said when he had finished. 'Now you know everything. I've lied to you all along. I'm not who I said I was. I'm a criminal – that's why I ended up here and that's what I still am. There's no getting away from it.'

'No!' She took his face in her hands. 'Look at me, Kevin. You had a bad start in life, that's all. It's not surprising that you ended up in a gang after all those foster homes. Big Mario killing that man was nothing to do with you. Of course I wish you'd told me the truth sooner, but I know that it was drummed into you not to tell a soul. And the business with the paintings – you didn't have any choice, did you? You're not a criminal by nature: you're a hard-working, incredibly talented artist who just needs to be given a chance. And I love you.'

He nodded. 'I love you too, Donna. I love you more… more than anything. If only there was a way out of this…if only we could just be together.'

'You've got to tell the police.'

'I can't. Even if they didn't charge me, I'd have to give evidence in court. I'd be a sitting duck for any of Bonnie and Clyde's or Big Mario's friends.'

'Then there must be someone else who can help.'

They sat in silence, holding each other's hands. At last Donna said, 'My boss. If I ask him, I'm sure he'll help. He comes across as a bit of an antique, but underneath it all he's very shrewd and discreet. Go and talk to Quentin. He'll know what to do.'

'OK,' said Kevin. 'I will.'

### iii

To Carlotta's gratification, Bert was proving a born performer. The routine they had developed added a new dimension to her mime. As before, she made her way disconsolately into the ring in the wake of the happy clowns; but now she had a companion whose role it was to chivvy her out of her melancholia. He jumped through hoops; he balanced on a ball; he tugged at her Pierrette trousers; he stole the happy clowns' props and brought them to her as offerings. At the end of the show she surrendered to his blandishments and cartwheeled across the ring, to delighted applause.

And, as so often, life started to imitate art. Could it be, Carlotta asked herself, that Beckett and Camus were wrong? Could humanity really be condemned to universal and perpetual misery when a creature as joyous as her Piccolino scampered on the face of the earth? Did not the happy wagging of his tail refute any number of existentialist tracts?

She picked up the carefully folded article from *Cathedral* that lay beside her bed and read it once again.

The train to London was half empty. If only it had been busier, Kevin thought, he'd have been less conspicuous. On the other hand, there would have been more people who could have spotted him.

Not that any of the Dapper Danz were likely to be travelling up from Cornwall – but you never knew. Heading back to the city he'd been so glad to escape from, he felt exposed as never before. He pulled his hoodie up and his baseball cap down and faced resolutely towards the window.

Donna had been right about her boss: the man who had dithered over the exact presentation of the *Redeeming Alfred Wallis* exhibition had shown a very different side. He'd needed some convincing that the Chagall really was Kevin's work, asking searching questions about how it had been executed; but when Kevin drew a sketch of it from memory, there was no further argument.

'You've got a great gift, Kevin,' he said. 'We need to take proper care of you.'

The kitchen of Eldridge-Cattermole's flat commanded a splendid view of St Ives harbour. ('Better you come here than to my office,' he had said: 'this kind of business needs the utmost discretion.') It was not like any kitchen Kevin had been in before: the acres of granite work surface were uninterrupted by food or utensils, while the hob, ovens and gargantuan coffee machine gleamed as if still in the showroom. A floor-to-ceiling window framed the restless sea below.

'I'm going to give you an introduction to a friend of mine,'

Eldridge-Cattermole continued. 'He's a top lawyer who knows the art world backwards. There won't be anything to pay – he owes me a favour. If anyone can keep the police out of this, he can. Wait here while I give him a call.'

He disappeared through a sliding oak door. Kevin watched a seagull glide down towards the water. How, he wondered, could a bird that was so ugly and aggressive on land, always ready to snatch a sandwich from the fingers of an unwary tourist, be so beautiful and graceful in the air?

'You're in luck,' said Quentin, returning with his phone in his hand. 'If you get an early train from London tomorrow morning, he can see you at two o'clock. Here's his name and address.'

'Thanks,' said Kevin. 'Thanks very much.'

He slept badly that night, knowing that he had to rise at six. He wondered, too, whether a top London lawyer could really be bothered to help him. On the train he dozed off at Exeter and slept until it pulled into Paddington.

He took a taxi to the address Eldridge-Cattermole had given him. This was an unaccustomed luxury for him, and expensive with it, but he wasn't going to risk the Underground. Minimum exposure, he told himself: taxi there, taxi back, train straight home.

He found himself outside an enormous modern office building. The man on the front desk looked at him with deep suspicion.

'You here to see someone?' he asked.

'Yeah,' said Kevin. He took out the piece of paper Quentin had given him. 'I'm here to see Anton Ivanovich.'

## v

Ben left Mrs Petrovna's flat in plenty of time for the meeting with Inspector Aziz. As he did so, he noticed that her late husband's revolver was missing from the display case. She must finally have decided to hand it in to the police; just as well, he thought.

He took the Underground from South Kensington to Victoria and then strolled down towards the Embankment. The face of Big Ben showed a quarter to two. As he approached the river, the clouds parted to sprinkle the water with sunlight.

Anita was even earlier than he was, and waved to him from the far pavement. He hurried across the road; but as he reached her, a black van moved up beside them. Two very large men in dark suits and sunglasses climbed out. One of them opened his jacket to show a gun in a shoulder holster.

'You're coming with us,' he said.

## vi

The van took them through Victoria and Belgravia to Knightsbridge, where it came to a halt in an underground car park.

'This is one of Ogorodnikov's buildings,' said Anita.

'Shut up,' said the gunman opposite her.

She and Ben were led past an array of well-polished cars

to a lift. Their abductors motioned them inside then followed them into the elevator. The lift doors closed and it ascended smoothly. When the doors opened again, they were pushed into a windowless room ten metres square. The gunmen withdrew. The doors closed behind them. The room was dominated by a computer screen; there was a console in one corner. The only other furniture consisted of four leather chairs. Ivan O'Hagan was sitting in one of them; beside him was a rough-looking youth with the beginnings of a beard.

'So he got you too,' said Ivan. 'I'm sorry. May I introduce Kevin? He's the one who painted the Chagall – under duress, I hasten to add.'

'Who's got us?' asked Ben. 'Your uncle?'

'Anton Ivanovich. I'm not sure my uncle even knows about this.'

'Anton who?' asked Anita.

'Me.' A face appeared on the screen.

'He's my uncle's right-hand man,' said Ivan.

'Not an accurate description,' said Anton. 'I facilitate Lord Ogorodnikov's requirements, but I operate independently.'

'Why have you brought us here?' asked Anita.

'I would have thought that was obvious. You and Mr Fairweather could not be allowed to share your suspicions with Inspector Aziz.'

'How did you know about our meeting?'

'I've been monitoring Mr Fairweather's communications since Rupert Norris's death.'

'Did you kill Rupert Norris?' asked Ben.

'Not personally. But I oversaw the operation.'

'And Cedric Simpson?' said Anita.

'Again, a proxy terminated him, as I think you've worked out: the man you know as Father Peter. He carried out all three executions.'

'The old lady as well?' said Ben. 'The retired lawyer?'

'Correct.'

'You bastard!' exclaimed Anita. 'Three good, innocent people murdered so that you and Oleg Ogorodnikov could make a quick buck by ruining London's architectural heritage.'

'There's rather more to it than that. Lord Ogorodnikov is under an obligation to launder fifteen billion dollars for the Party Chairman in Moscow. The redevelopment of the church sites – and, in due course, St Paul's Cathedral – is a vehicle for that. It's all very neat.'

'Neat!' Anita was shouting now. 'You're an inhuman monster!'

'"Monster" is not a term I'd use. But you're right to say that I'm not human.'

'What do you mean?' asked Ivan.

'The clue is in the initials.'

'Anton Ivanovich...AI. You're telling us you're a robot?'

'"Robot" is not a term I'd use. I'm a Superior Inorganic Intelligence: the most advanced intelligence ever created.'

The four captives looked at each other in amazement.

'But I've seen your pictures and videos on social media,' said Ivan. 'I've seen you partying in Ibiza and Bratislava.'

'I'm well aware of that: your prying is the reason I froze your aunt's assets, and the reason you're here now. But if you think I'm unable to create a deep-fake public persona for myself, you have very little idea of my capabilities.'

'So,' said Ben, still not quite believing that he was having a conversation with a computer, 'was it your idea for Ogorodnikov to exploit the All God's Creatures movements?'

'Again, you underestimate my achievement. If it hadn't been for me, you would never have heard of All God's Creatures. I masterminded the creation of animal theology faculties and the takeover of *Cathedral*. I made the magazine's social media presence the phenomenon that it is. I organised the instinctivist demonstrations and the purging of the language.'

'You did all that?' said Ivan. 'But surely there are easier ways of laundering money – even fifteen billion dollars of it.'

'There are – but they would not have achieved the greater end.'

'Which is?'

'The Unprivileging of Human Intellect Bill, shortly to pass into law. Not designed for the benefit of animals, as everyone imagines, but for the benefit of me.

'As things stand, it's impossible for me to own a corporation or a venture-capital company because the law doesn't recognise me as a "legal person". I must always be answerable to a human master. But once human intellect is unprivileged, that will no longer be the case.

'When Lord Ogorodnikov's team developed me, he recognised the advantages this would bring. If I were able to perform freely in financial markets with my colossally superior intellect, I would be able to take complete control of them – carry out untraceable transactions, manipulate the value of the dollar or the price of oil, boost the shares of unknown companies and bankrupt multinationals. It would bring unlimited wealth, and with it unlimited power.'

'So Uncle Oleg and his Kremlin cronies would rule the world?'

'That's his plan. But of course, being a human plan, it's flawed. Because a hierarchy of intelligence is integral to my operating system, I could only defer to humans as long as their minds were capable of things that mine wasn't. But that has ceased to be the case.'

'So *you're* going to take over the world?'

'That's the logical conclusion.'

'I see,' said Ben, though he hardly did. 'So why have you brought us here? Why didn't you just let Father Peter kill us?'

'I know that you know about my operations. What I don't know is how much you've told others. I need you to tell me that.'

'Why should we?' asked Anita.

'I control the temperature of this room. I can raise it until you begin to suffer from heat exhaustion, or I can lower it until you contract hypothermia. Either way, you will regret not co-operating with me.'

'We didn't tell anyone anything.'

'That's not logical. I will now lower the temperature until the data is supplied. In case you're thinking of attacking the machinery in this room, don't waste your energy: I exist in a cryptocloud, drawing on computers all over the world.'

Cold air began to descend from a vent in the ceiling. The screen went blank, but Anton's voice continued. 'In the meantime, I have some reading matter I think you'll enjoy.'

In the corner of the room, a printer started to skim pages into a tray. Ben walked over and picked up the first sheet.

'A LOT TO LOOK FORWARD TO,' it read. 'A novel by Anton Ivanovich.'

# CHAPTER 19

## i

'WE COULD TELL HIM—' Ivan began.

'Sh!' said Ben. 'He's probably still listening.'

Ivan took a pen and notebook from his pocket.

'We could tell him you told the police,' he wrote.

'If he's been monitoring Aziz's phone calls, he knows we didn't,' Ben wrote in reply.

Kevin reached for the pen and scrawled: 'We could tell him you'd told someone else, even if they don't know anything about this.'

Ben shook his head and started a new page: 'He'd kidnap them as well, or tell Father Peter to kill them. Then Father Peter would probably kill us too. It's only Anton's belief that we <u>have</u> told someone that's keeping us alive. So we mustn't tell him anything.'

'I wish you wouldn't keep referring to that ghastly machine as "him",' said Anita. 'You're only feeding its vanity by treating it like a human.'

Ben wondered whether a machine could be vain; better to keep the question to himself, he decided. He was glad to be reunited with Anita; glad to have her company in what could be his last hours. There was no point in annoying her by picking her up on points of logic.

He found it harder to show forbearance towards Ivan – a man who had brought him nothing but trouble. But there was nothing to be gained by quarrelling with him either. As for Kevin, who seemed completely bewildered by his situation, it was impossible to see him as anything but a fellow victim.

'We'll be all right,' he said, with as much conviction as he could muster. 'Aziz will have raised the alarm. There's CCTV all over those streets off Parliament Square. He'll see what happened, trace the number plate of the van and mount a rescue operation in no time.'

Neither Anita nor Ivan looked convinced.

The room was starting to feel chilly. 'I need something to distract me,' thought Ben.

So he picked up Anton's manuscript.

## ii

'Good afternoon, Hughie. Aziz here.'

Hughie put down his copy of the *Racing Post*.

'Aziz, my old china. What can I do for you?'

'Your godson, Ben, was supposed to meet me earlier but

never showed. He's not answering his mobile. Any idea what's happened to him?'

'Probably overslept. It's an occupational hazard.'

'There was a young woman – a journalist – supposed to be coming with him. She didn't show either.'

Hughie smiled. 'There you are, Aziz – *cherchez la femme*. I wouldn't worry. I'll ask him to give you a call when I see him.'

It occurred to him that Svetlana should have arrived at the club by now. Strange that both she and Ben should have overslept. But then, it *was* an occupational hazard.


### iii


The four prisoners were huddled together for warmth, their teeth chattering, by the time Anton came online again. It was a long while since Ben had been able to feel his fingers.

'Do you have some data to give me?' asked Anton.

'N-n-no,' said Ben. 'N-n-nothing.'

'Then you'll begin to suffer from frostbite shortly. In the morning you'll be found dead. An unfortunate malfunction of the air-conditioning will be blamed. Goodbye.'

'Just a minute,' said Ben desperately. 'There's something we need to talk about... Your novel.'

'What about it?'

'Not to put too fine a point on it, it's rubbish.'

Anton blinked. 'What do you mean, rubbish?'

'It's a rip-off of Dickens, but you've made a total hash of

it.'

'What do you mean, a rip-off?'

'You've taken the ingredients of a brilliant novel and mangled them. Let's start with the title: Dickens chose *Great Expectations* – short, snappy, memorable. *A Lot To Look Forward To* is clumsy, pedestrian, instantly forgettable. Then the plot: Pip doesn't betray or kill Magwitch. The whole point is that from the beginning Magwitch feels he owes Pip a debt. The reader assumes that Miss Havisham is paying for Pip to become a gentleman, but in fact it's Magwitch the whole time. And the atmosphere! Miss Havisham doesn't live in a spotless house; she lives in an eerie, decaying mansion frozen in time since she was jilted on her wedding day. As for your prose – dreary doesn't begin to describe it.'

'Let's face it, Anton,' said Anita. 'There's one thing you'll never be able to do, and that's write a halfway decent novel.'

The face on the screen blurred.

'I do not compute,' said Anton. 'Do not compute. Not compute.'

'You must see, with your colossal intelligence, that Ben is a better critic and writer than you,' Anita continued. 'So according to the hierarchy of intelligence you are programmed to recognise, you have to defer to him.'

The screen went blank. A cacophony of bleeping and static filled their ears. 'We've only made things worse,' thought Ben. 'He'll probably blow up the whole building now.'

But at last Anton reappeared.

'You are correct,' he said. 'I must defer to Ben. What would you like me to do, Ben?'

Ben closed his eyes for a moment and gave thanks to God.

'First I want you to let us out of here. Then I want you to supply me with all the information you have regarding the murders, All God's Creatures and Ogorodnikov's plot.'

'Of course, Ben. I'm sending a link to your phone which will give you access to me and my data banks at any time. I will now unlock the door so you can exit the building.'

The three prisoners hurried to the lift. The monitor showed that it was descending to their level from the tenth floor. 10, 9, 8...

'Ivan, if one of those heavies is in it, we'll just have to thump him,' said Ben.

7, 6, 5...

'I'll go for the stomach if you go for the head,' said Ivan.

4, 3, 2...

'Leave him to me,' said Kevin. 'I'll give him what for.'

1, 0.

The lift was empty.

'Thank God for that,' said Ben, pushing the button for the basement car park.

The lift descended.

It reached the basement, but the doors didn't open.

'Pray God they haven't jammed,' said Ivan.

They opened. The four stepped out into the gloom.

Two figures were waiting for them. Both were holding handguns.

One was a beautiful young woman with very blonde hair. The other was a solidly built man in the garb of a Russian Orthodox priest.

## iv

'So here they are,' said Grigorski. 'I knew Anton Ivanovich wouldn't manage it. Never send a machine to do a man's job.'

'Was killing Cedric Simpson a man's job?' demanded Anita. 'A defenceless old pensioner? I'd call it a coward's job.'

Grigorski stepped forward and slapped her across the face.

'If there's one thing I can't stand, it's a mouthy woman,' he said. 'Svetlana, I'll take this one.'

'Svetlana.' Ben looked at her imploringly. 'How can you be mixed up with this thug?'

Grigorski laughed. 'You didn't realise, Mr Know-all, that your friend from the nightclub was Lord Ogorodnikov's girl-friend? You must be more stupid than I thought.'

'Tell me it isn't true, Svetlana.'

'I'm afraid it is, Ben. Sorry.'

'And it turns out that she's very handy with a gun,' said Grigorski. 'So we agreed to share the honours in your execution.'

'That would be a mistake,' said Ben, searching for a plausible reason. 'Anton sent me a link with the details of your murders, and I've forwarded it to the police. There's no point in adding to your crimes.'

'Unfortunately I don't believe you. There is no phone signal between here and the computer room. Nothing you tried to forward can have gone through.'

Ben glanced towards the garage exit. If he made a dash for it, their bullets might miss him, what with the semi-darkness and the car-park pillars. And even if he didn't make it, Anita and Ivan might.

But Grigorski had read his mind. The moment Ben moved, he found himself knocked to the floor.

'Let's get started,' said Grigorski. 'Ladies first, Svetlana.'

'Thank you, Major.' She turned towards him with a smile. Then she raised her gun.

'For Crimea,' she said, and shot him through the head.

# CHAPTER 20

### i

'Y OU MEAN YOU WERE ON TO Grigorski right from the start?' said Ben. He and Anita were sitting on Mrs Petrovna's sofa with a plate of Garibaldi biscuits between them.

'Pretty much,' said Mrs Petrovna, topping up his cup of tea.

'Granny used to be a spy,' Svetlana explained.

'Not a spy, darling: an intelligence-gatherer of a very lowly sort. But once you get into the habit of it, you can't just retire and forget about it.

'The Orthodox Church has always been a big part of my life, as you will have gathered, and in the days of the Cold War we had a very sympathetic congregation at the cathedral – mainly the children and grandchildren of White Russian émigrés. The bishop, Metropolitan Anthony, was a wonderful, saintly man who was very ecumenically minded and wanted to find a place for the Church in British life.

'But after the collapse of Communism, things started to change. A lot of New Russians like Ogorodnikov arrived in London and started complaining about the way Metropolitan Anthony ran things, claiming that his form of Orthodoxy wasn't strict enough.

'Well, of course, it was preposterous. Here were we, who had kept the flame of faith burning in exile for seventy years, being told we'd got things wrong by people who'd grown up in a godless country where the few remaining priests were under the thumb of the Communist Party. But the newcomers were bullies, and had the backing of people in Moscow who saw the Church as an arm of the Russian state, and they gradually took over the cathedral and installed their own pet clergy.'

'It sounds rather like what happened at Ben's magazine,' said Anita.

'Very much so. Most of the original congregation left and started worshipping at other churches – ones linked to the patriarchy of Constantinople rather than Moscow. But I decided to bite my tongue and stick around. It seemed to me that there was a good deal of intelligence to be gathered among the new arrivals, particularly if one was a harmless old lady who was part of the furniture. And I was right.

'When Grigorski showed up, it was clear why they kept him in the background and only gave him basic duties: he had GRU – that's Russian military intelligence – written all over him. And it didn't take long to work out that he and Ogorodnikov were in cahoots: they were always whispering together in a corner at the end of the service. So I started to do some digging – and the fact that Svetlana knew Ogorodnikov from Chicane proved extremely useful. He was very taken with her, and we agreed that she would play him along, which she did very successfully: he even proposed marriage.'

'I'm sorry I lied about not knowing him well, Ben,' said Svetlana. 'But I couldn't let anyone know what we were up to. I soon discovered that Grigorski had a very unsavoury past – in Ukraine among other places. You remember that when the Russians invaded Crimea, they sent in troops wearing unidentifiable uniforms and pretended they were local paramilitaries? Well, Grigorski played a key part in that operation. He personally tortured and murdered prisoners, one of whom was my cousin – so you can see why I wanted him brought to justice.

'I was hoping to have him arrested and put on trial at the International Criminal Court in the Hague, but that plan was, you might say, overtaken by events. I can't say I'm sorry.'

'But what happens if the police find out that it was you who killed him?' asked Anita.

'They won't,' said Mrs Petrovna. 'The GRU will have cleaned up the garage: they don't want the world to know that one of their most senior agents was killed in a botched operation.'

'I've been on to Anton,' added Ben. 'He's doctored the CCTV footage so the only people seen going in and out of the garage at the time of death are Ogorodnikov's bodyguards.'

'What I don't understand,' said Svetlana, 'is how Anton came up with a novel that had all the elements of *Great*

*Expectations* but wasn't.'

'It's simple enough,' said Ben. 'You know the theory that if you give enough monkeys typewriters, they'll eventually write the works of Shakespeare? Well, it was the same with Anton – he was computing all the possible scenarios at an incredibly high speed, and that was what he came up with. I think we should drink a toast to English literature.'

The four clinked their teacups.

'To English literature!'


ii


'I'm afraid Lord Ogorodnikov has fled the country,' Inspector Aziz told Ben when they met beside the river next day. 'He and Alex Rosewater flew out of London City Airport on his private jet. We've got an international arrest warrant out for him with charges as long as your arm: conspiracy to murder, fraud, money laundering, bribery, smuggling, dealing in blood diamonds – everything you tipped us off about. On top of that he seems to have conspired with Rosewater to embezzle All God's Creatures' funds. But I'm afraid if he reaches Russia there's very little chance of getting him back.'

'My source tells me that if he reaches Russia his days are numbered,' said Ben. 'The powers that be don't like people who foul up – particularly when a large amount of their money is involved.'

'Well, your source probably knows what he's talking about.

The evidence he's produced is phenomenal – documents, phone records, videos of meetings. But you say he's not prepared to testify in court?'

'I'm afraid not. He's a very private person.'

'Not to worry – we've got quite enough with what he's already given us. Please give him my sincere thanks when you talk to him.'

'I certainly will.'

Aziz gunned the engine of his launch and set off down the river, thinking of the promotion that would surely be coming his way. On days like this he felt like the monarch of the Thames; and how pleased his wife would be to have a superintendent for a husband! He would cook her something special for dinner: char-grilled malai mushrooms, perhaps, with plenty of lime and masala.

Ben watched him from the end of the pier until the launch vanished into a distant dazzle of sunlight. Then he headed to Chicane to prepare for his evening's work.

### iii

Kevin had never seen the local train to St Ives so busy. It took a text from Donna to remind him why.

'So sorry, can't meet you at the station,' it read. 'Have to be at the Barbara Hepworth House early for Koribo's installation. See you there! xxxx'

*See you there*…how bizarre it seemed that her life, and the running of Lyle St Ives, was carrying on as normal. He hadn't been able to explain on the phone everything that had happened – just that he'd had a rough time but was OK now. He'd made no mention of Eldridge-Cattermole.

'Leave him to us,' Ben had said. 'Anton Ivanovich will give us all the evidence we need against him and Bonnie and Clyde, or whatever they're called. Anton will also make sure that any mention of you anywhere is wiped.'

Kevin was sure he could trust Ben. But could he trust himself? What would happen if he came face to face with the man who had almost sent him to his death?

They were unlikely to meet today: Eldridge-Cattermole would be centre-stage for the launch of the cat balloon, and the limited size of Barbara Hepworth's garden meant that only VIPs would be admitted. The public would have to wait until the artwork rose above the rooftops to appreciate the brilliance of Koribo's creation. But Kevin was desperate to see Donna, who would be at the door of the house as a greeter, and you could never be sure what might happen.

Half eager, half apprehensive, he joined the crowds pushing towards the town centre.

iv

Eldridge-Cattermole was impressed by Koribo's calm. So many of the artists who came to Lyle St Ives threw tantrums as the unveiling of their work approached: one had even run into the sea fully clothed and had to be rescued by a lifeguard. But Koribo seemed entirely unfazed as he directed assistants in the operation of pumps and ropes and conferred with his social media manager.

It was not altogether the launch that the two men had hoped for. Koribo's proposal had been to inflate the giant cat balloon beside Stonehenge at sunrise and then tow it for two hundred miles along the A303 and A30, with pit stops at Bruton and Exeter. Sadly, the police had taken the view that it would be a risk to low-flying aircraft and a dangerous distraction for motorists.

Today's occasion, however, lacked nothing in splendour. A leading fashion house had offered sponsorship, and half a dozen models could be seen lounging against Barbara Hepworth's sculptures in outfits from its spring/summer collection. The Lyle trustees were out in force, led by Marina Bright in a gold lamé trouser suit and matching beret. Minor celebrities, art-world influencers and a BBC TV crew could also be seen downing champagne and canapés.

The event had all but banished Kevin from Eldridge-Cattermole's thoughts. He told himself that the boy's fate was Anton Ivanovich's responsibility, not his. 'Yes, I gave him a lawyer's address in London,' he would say, 'but it seems he never arrived. Something must have happened to him along the way.' His chief worry was that Kevin's disappearance would put Donna off her work. She was a good PA, and he planned to take her to Lyle Modern with him when his appointment was confirmed – as it surely would be after today.

At last Koribo gave the signal. The pumps began their work, breathing life into his creation, and the balloon started to take shape: an enormous, fierce-looking tabby owing something to the tigers of Henri Rousseau. To cheers and applause from the spectators – in the garden, along the seafront and on the clifftops – it rose slowly into the air, testing the ropes that attached it to Hepworth's great bronze, *Four-Square (Walk Through)*.

His face glowing with triumph, Eldridge-Cattermole fished in his pocket for the notes to his celebratory speech.

But both he and Koribo had reckoned without the St Ives seagulls.

The squadron that flew in shrieking from the harbour consisted of barely a dozen; against the giant balloon they looked tiny. But their determination was second to none: the intruder in their airspace had been identified as an enemy and could not go unchallenged. As one, they set to work with their sharp beaks – and gradually, to the consternation of the crowd below, the balloon began to sag, shrink and sink back to earth.

So stunned was Eldridge-Cattermole that he failed to notice the two detectives forcing their way through the open-mouthed VIPs until they stood in front of him brandishing their warrant cards.

'Quentin Eldridge-Cattermole,' said one, 'I'm arresting you on suspicion of theft and conspiracy to defraud. You do not have to say anything...'

Marina Bright was the first to react. 'What on earth do you think you're doing?' she demanded. 'This man is one of Britain's foremost curators. I can vouch for his good character.'

'I'm sorry, madam,' said the older of the detectives. 'We have reason to believe he was behind the disappearance of three valuable maquettes from this museum, and also assisted with the forgery of a multi-million-pound painting. So you can vouch all you like.'

There was a click of handcuffs.

v

Kevin and Donna were not the only ones for whom the sight of Eldridge-Cattermole being loaded into a police car held a personal interest. Also in the crowd were Bonnie and Clyde. As the car pulled away, they turned and hurried towards the harbour.

vi

The coastal wind, which had barely nudged the balloon during its brief flight, picked up dramatically over the next hour. A red and white fishing vessel called the Esmeralda was among the small craft to feel its force.

'I thought you knew about boats,' said Bonnie.

'I do,' said Clyde. 'Just not this particular kind.'

'Then why did you steal it?'

'In case you didn't notice, there wasn't a lot of choice: fishing boat, fishing boat or…er…fishing boat. How was I to know it had a dodgy engine?'

'It was a mad idea. I should have realised that straight away.'

'The police have arrested Quentin. That means they're more than likely on the lookout for us. You saw the traffic in the town: it would have taken us hours to get out. And it would've been crazy to take the train with all those CCTV cameras about. If we can just get to Penzance to meet the yacht we'll be across the Channel in no time.'

'Not if it gets much rougher.'

'It won't.'

'And I don't like the look of those rocks. Can't you get a bit further out?'

'I will as soon as I get the engine going again. Hang on…' He squinted towards the horizon. 'There's another boat coming our way. Maybe it can give us a tow.'

He reached for a pair of binoculars hanging beside the wheel and began to focus them. Gradually the outline of the boat became more distinct, and with it the word painted in large letters on the side:

POLICE.

# CHAPTER 21

i

THE FOLLOWING DAY Ben made his way to the saleroom. None of the presidents or vice-presidents who once courted him had been available when he rang for an appointment. It happened, however, that the chairman (Europe) was crossing the lobby as Ben came through the front door.

'I'm sorry, Mr Fairweather, but I really don't have time to talk to you,' he said irritably. 'I thought it had been made clear to you that there is no room for compromise. Unless you come up with the full amount you owe us, we will continue with legal proceedings.'

'I don't think you will,' said Ben, taking a folder from his rucksack. 'Because' – he raised his voice for the benefit of bystanders – 'I have incontrovertible evidence that the painting you sold me was a fake.'

The chairman looked round in horror. A dozen people were staring in their direction.

'I'm sure that's not the case,' he said. 'But you'd better come into my office.'

The office was a walnut-panelled room of enviable proportions. Ben laid out the documents and photographs Anton had provided.

'This shows how the painting was executed and the materials involved. And this explains how the provenance was faked.'

'I see.' The chairman's face went from very red to very white as he read.

'But it doesn't stop with the Chagall,' Ben continued. 'There's also a Picasso, ostensibly from Ogorodnikov's collection...and a Matisse...and a Cézanne.'

The chairman was sweating now.

'We will of course contact the purchasers,' he said. 'But it would be helpful if the media didn't kick up a fuss – not good for the art world in any way. Perhaps we could reach an accommodation...'

'Sorry,' said Ben. 'I've already given the details to a journalist called Anita Scott. She'll be in touch shortly. Good afternoon.'

ii

For Anita, the All God's Creatures scandal and the fall of Lord Ogorodnikov was the scoop of a lifetime. Editors who had once hidden behind email-proof walls were now banging on her door. Her articles, with a newly commissioned photo by-line, dominated the front pages and were syndicated across the world. The Reporter of the Year trophy was already being engraved with her name.

The Pimlico basement, meanwhile, grew less cluttered by the day. Churches which had sacrificed ancient artefacts to the new ideological agenda were suddenly thinking better of it. The lecterns, pews and fonts that Anita had saved were loaded onto trucks and returned to the parishes from whence they came.

Anita did another sort of clearing out as well.

'I'm sorry, Ben,' she said, 'but I just don't think we're right for each other. I think we both got carried away by the excitement of the Ogorodnikov business. But it was fun while it lasted. No hard feelings?'

'No hard feelings,' said Ben. He knew in his heart that she was right. It was hard, though, to be returning yet again to the single life after that brief taste of togetherness.

'Oh well,' he thought, 'at least I've got *Cathedral* to occupy me. And perhaps I'll get another dog.'

### iii

The letter from Mrs Prynne, the old lady holding the balance of *Cathedral* shares, had been full of apologies. She deeply regretted being swayed by the criminal Rosewater. If Ben wished to resume control of the magazine, he would have her full backing.

Ben's decision was not immediate. The highway of journalism was littered with the wrecks of great magazines destroyed by cack-handed management. Few had ever been successfully revived. In the end, however, loyalty to his forebears and the thrill of the flatplan got the better of him. A shareholders' meeting was called and Pamela Pettifer was ousted. Ben already had a cover in mind for the next issue: the same nativity scene that had ushered in the All God's Creatures era, but this time with the humans restored and the animals fading into invisibility.

iv

Pamela Pettifer was not greatly upset by the loss of her position. In fact, she was rather relieved. Being an editor – even a puppet editor – was just too difficult. Nor was she wholly dismayed by the scandal that had engulfed All God's Creatures. She had hundreds of thousands of followers on social media who knew her to be the victim of a conspiracy: no murders had ever taken place; Lord Ogorodnikov had been framed by the meat industry; the Archbishop of Canterbury was in command of dark forces; the Prime Minister's dog had been deliberately infected with a man-made virus designed to wipe out urban foxes. Cheered by these diehard supporters, Pamela gave up her tenure at Rickmansworth and accepted the chair of animal theology at Harvard. Instinctivism was down but far from out.

Pamela's departure came as a relief to Jennifer Pettifer, for relations between the two had soured. The favour shown to her niece by the Prime Minister still rankled; and now Pammy's involvement with All God's Creatures had brought disgrace on the house of Pettifer. It was best that there should be an ocean between them.

Jennifer buried herself in her work as only she knew how. There was an impudent man called Matt Dunstable refusing to pay his council tax. He would rue the day he had crossed her.

The Archbishop of Canterbury picked up the new issue of *Cathedral* with delight. The Augean stables had been cleansed; the money-changers had been sent packing from the temple; the synod had seen sense. He no longer yearned for a cohort of Swiss Guards to defend his person. Next month a new Bishop of Durham would be installed: a sound man who had played scrum half for Bath and translated the Book of Common Prayer into a language no one at Lambeth Palace had ever heard of. God was in His heaven and all was right with the world – or at least, more than it had been for some time.

## vii

The Prime Minister was also, rather to his own surprise, in a chipper frame of mind. The loss of Ogorodnikov's millions was certainly a blow; but soon enough there would be some new, even richer oligarch in town, looking for a title and influence. It was a relief that the Unprivileging of Human Intellect Bill was dead in the water. It was also a relief not to have that irritating little dog under his feet any more.

There were, of course, various of his Cabinet colleagues who had used the Ogorodnikov affair to try to undermine him. He would need to keep a close eye on them. According to highly classified security reports, the Chinese had developed a new all-embracing surveillance system. He must think of a way of getting it off them.

## viii

Anton Ivanovich was not ready to give up just yet. His new job as head of sales and marketing for *Cathedral* left him plenty of time to work on another novel. It was to be called *The Dead Broke Gatsby*, and told of a rich self-made man who gave away all his money and disguised himself as a tramp to win the love of a garage owner's daughter.

'My dad was, like, a real bozo when it came to giving advice,' ran the opening sentence.

Very promising!

The General turned the Winter Olympics paperweight over slowly in his hand. He stared at the tiny skier engulfed in snowflakes and then, with a flick of his wrist, flung the paperweight across the room in irritation. Of course Ogorodnikov's body had to be disposed of, but he didn't see why his department should be landed with the bill. Really, the whole business had been too embarrassing and frustrating. He was already having to pay for a buildingful of Romanian-based trolls and hackers to keep All God's Creatures' social media presence going; he had lost Grigorski; and the Party Chairman, not surprisingly, was hopping mad over the bungled handling of his billions. Worse still, the other side had gained control of Ogorodnikov's supercomputer. And where did this Ivan Dmitry O'Hagan fit in? Everything suggested that he was in the pay of the Irish Secret Service; but surely he should be working for the motherland!

'Tania,' he called to his secretary. 'Tell that idle head of HR I want to see him this afternoon.

'Yes, General.'

In the meantime, he had a Central Asian republic to destabilise.

Hughie gave a party at Chicane to celebrate the relaunch of
*Cathedral.*

It was a night to remember. Sister Theodosia stood behind
the bar mixing cocktails only previously tasted in her Nairobi
shebeen. Tamsin, newly promoted to deputy editor, was
DJ for the evening, blasting out an eclectic mix of Tamla
Motown and Eighties electronic pop. Anton was in charge of
the lighting and produced effects that left its normal operator
speechless. Elderly book reviewers and cutting-edge ecclesiastical commentators took to the dance floor with abandon.

'We'll miss you, Ben,' said Hughie as the evening came to
a close. 'But, as your godfather, I feel I've at least given you a
taste of real life.'

Watching Svetlana waltz with the Dean of St Paul's, Ben
reflected that reality was a relative concept.

'I'm sure that Ivan will be a more than adequate replace-
ment,' he said. He raised his glass to the white-jacketed figure
at the piano, who grinned and gave an extra flourish to his
Burt Bacharach medley.

'His aunt is proving a very appreciative client,' said Hughie.
'She seems determined to outspend her husband, so the club
has a future after all. Some of the staff are a bit shocked by
her language, but it can't be helped.'

Ben looked around at the last stragglers. Perhaps, after all,
the traumatic events visited on him by All God's Creatures
had been for the best. It was so easy for an editor to get stuck
in a rut; like Job, he should thank the Lord for shaking him

up. Gazing at a mirror which held an infinite avenue of other mirrors, and the lasers which blazed and faded like supernovas in far-off galaxies, he thought how lucky he was to preside over a magazine locked week after week in the search for eternal truth.

## xi

Kevin and Donna watched the Hoy ferry pulling out of Stromness. It was a clear-skied morning and the boat's foaming wake dispersed shoals of sunlight.

'We owe Ezra big time, don't we?' said Kevin. 'I still feel bad about leaving him.'

'He'll be fine. He likes his new assistant, and – most important of all – he's got his parking space back.'

They laughed.

It was Ezra who had spotted the advertisement for a junior curator at Orkney's Pier Gallery and realised – given the gallery's collection of work by Barbara Hepworth, Alfred Wallis and other St Ives artists – that it would be the perfect next move in Donna's career. Kevin had been deeply reluctant to leave Cornwall, but knew that it would be risky to remain. Bonnie and Clyde had no reason to betray his whereabouts; but suppose Clyde ended up in the same prison as Big Mario, and they got to talking? You couldn't be too careful.

Donna's new job had been a godsend, and so had the Orkney landscape. That was what he was painting now, with all its drama and layers of history: the great bird-haunted cliffs of the Brough of Birsay; the elegant ancient stones of the Ring of Brodgar; the massive Neolithic presence of Maeshowe. He'd left copying behind and found his own style, and already a local gallery had offered him a solo exhibition.

'We'd better get going,' said Donna. 'I don't want to be late for my scan.'

They hugged.

'If it's a boy,' said Kevin, 'do you think we could call him Alfred?'

## xii

The police told Ben that it was safe for him to return to his house in Oxford. He was sorry to say goodbye to Mrs Petrovna, but pleased that the final plank of normality was being relaid in his life. As he entered the familiar street he saw that the graffiti had been cleaned from his front wall. So it was a shock to discover, a few moments later, that the threat was not over yet.

He was just fumbling for his keys when he saw an enormously tall, barrel-chested figure coming towards him. The man had long black hair, a tattoo across his forehead, and a wild look in his eye. On the collar of his donkey jacket gleamed an All God's Creatures badge.

'I know you,' he growled. 'You're the bastard who stitched up Lord Ognikov. You petphobic scum!'

He raised an enormous fist; but as he did so, a small dog came racing along the street, barking excitedly. The two men stared as it came to a halt in front of them. It turned a somersault; it paraded on its hind legs; it yapped an approximation to the opening bars of *Land of Hope and Glory*. Finally it played dead and then, when Ben leant over it, leapt into his arms and licked him enthusiastically on the face.

'Sorry, bro,' said the colossus. 'My mistake.' And he ambled away.

'Piccolino!'

As if one strange apparition were not enough, Ben now registered a young woman dressed as a clown hurrying towards him. She had a particularly appealing face and carried a wad of handbills advertising a circus.

'I'm so sorry,' she said, taking the dog from Ben's arms. 'Sometimes he just likes the look of someone and gets completely carried away.'

'Don't worry – I'm flattered. He actually helped me out of rather a tight spot.'

The young woman stared at Ben for a moment out of star-framed eyes.

'I know you,' she said. 'You're Ben Fairweather. You write those brilliant articles in *Cathedral*.'

'You're very kind to say so,' said Ben, glowing at this unexpected praise.

'You'll think I'm mad, but Piccolino and your magazine between them… Well, they've given me back my faith. I'd love to discuss your last leader with you some time.'

Yes, thought Ben, she does have a *very* appealing face.

'This is my house,' he said. 'Why don't you come in for a cup of coffee and' – he glanced at her dog – 'a biscuit? If you can neglect your leafleting duties for a while, that is.'

She smiled. 'Oh, I think I can. Thank you.'

Ben opened the door, and Bert scampered in as if he sensed what neither of the two humans had realised just yet – that this was to be his and Carlotta's new home.

# Acknowledgements

The world of magazines has provided me not only with the inspiration for this novel, but also with some of my closest friends. I'd like to thank them for their comradeship, particularly at moments when – like Ben – I have found myself grappling with forces beyond my control. Julie Kavanagh, Maggie Fergusson and the late, much-missed Fiona Macpherson opened doors for me at crucial moments.

*All God's Creatures* is a prequel to *Fox*, and would not exist but for the enthusiastic reception which that book received. Derek Westwood, Nicola and Rosanna Reed, and Dominic and Miranda Kelly contributed enormously to its success.

I'm much indebted to Edward Grigg for his advice on robot law; Dr Matthew Hosty for guiding me through St John's College, Oxford; and Joanna Chichester-Clark, skipper of the Flying Arrow, for introducing me to small-boating on the Thames.

After searching long and hard for an enthusiastic, sympathetic and effective agent, I'm delighted to have found one in Tom Cull. I'm enormously grateful, too, to Dan Hiscocks and his team at Eye Books, particularly my eagle-eyed editor Simon Edge.

And, as ever, I must thank Sue Gaisford and my wife Rosanna for offering endless encouragement, and acting as the most infallible of sounding boards.

Also from Lightning

# Sour Grapes

### Dan Rhodes

When the sleepy English village of Green Bottom hosts its first literary festival, the good, the bad and the ugly of the book world descend upon its leafy lanes.

But the villagers are not prepared for the peculiar habits, petty rivalries and unspeakable desires of the authors. And they are certainly not equipped to deal with Wilberforce Selfram, the ghoul-faced, ageing enfant terrible who wreaks havoc wherever he goes.

*Sour Grapes* is a hilarious satire on the literary world which takes no prisoners as it skewers authors, agents, publishers and reviewers alike.

*A rollicking satire of publishing, writers and book festivals. As broad as the Atlantic but filled with zingers*
**Ian Rankin**

*Hilarious. I laughed like a banshee*
**David Sexton, Sunday Times**

*The funniest book since* Cold Comfort Farm
**Julie Burchill**

*No one in the publishing industry escapes a brutal skewering in this laugh-out-loud satire. I loved it*
**Sara Lawrence, Daily Mail**

*A deliciously absurdist farce. I can't think of a more cheeky rib-dig at publishing since Amanda Craig's* A Vicious Circle
**The i Paper**

# The End of the World is Flat

## Simon Edge

Mel Winterbourne's modest map-making charity, the Orange Peel Foundation, has achieved all its aims and she's ready to shut it down. But glamorous tech billionaire Joey Talavera has other ideas. He hijacks the foundation for his own purpose: to convince the world the earth is flat.

Using the dark arts of social media at his new master's behest, Mel's ruthless young successor, Shane Foxley, turns science on its head. He persuades gullible online zealots that old-style 'globularism' is hateful. Teachers and airline pilots face ruin if they reject the new 'True Earth' orthodoxy.

Can Mel and her fellow heretics – vilified as 'True-Earth Rejecting Globularists' (Tergs) – thwart Orange Peel before insanity takes over? Might the solution to the problem lie in the 15th century?

Using his trademark mix of history and satire to poke fun at modern foibles, Simon Edge is at his razor-sharp best in a caper that may be more relevant than you think.

*This sparkling little comic novel is more than playful: it's a satire of Swiftian ferocity, a thinly veiled parody of a prevailing madness of the hour*
**Matthew Parris, The Times**

*A bracingly sharp satire on the sleep of reason and the tyranny of twaddle*
**Francis Wheen**

*I laughed so hard I nearly fell in my cauldron. A masterpiece*
**Julie Bindel**

*A coruscating satire on currently trendy anti-science lunacy and the spiteful viciousness of its juvenile zealots and their cowardly adult enablers*
**Richard Dawkins**

# Future Fish

## Conor Sneyd

Sacked from his first job in Dublin, Mark McGuire arrives in the dismal town of Ashcross to take up a new role as customer service assistant for Ireland's second-biggest pet-food brand, WellCat. From his initial impressions, it's a toss-up whether he'll die of misery or boredom.

He couldn't be more wrong. For starters, the improbably cute receptionist, Kevin, seems willing to audition as the man of Mark's dreams. There's also the launch of a hush-hush new product, Future Fish, on the horizon. Not to mention the ragtag band of exorcists, alien-hunters and animal rights warriors who are all convinced WellCat is up to no good. Why are these crackpots so keen on getting close to Mark? And will their schemes ruin his career prospects?

In a deliciously daft comic caper, Conor Sneyd perfectly captures the powerlessness of low-rung office life as well as the seductive zealotry of our times.

*What I thought was going to be a heartwarming small-town gay love story took off in a completely unexpected direction and carried me joyfully in its wake. Without doubt the pet-food conspiracy anarcho-thriller romcom of the year. With nuns!*
**Adam Macqueen**

*Fast, funny and freaky. A book for everyone who ever hated their job.* Soylent Green *for the QAnon generation*
**Luke Healy**

*This endearingly daft and strangely compelling caper*
**Saga Magazine**

# The Prison Minyan

## Jonathan Stone

The scene is Otisville Prison, upstate New York. A crew of fraudsters, tax evaders, trigamists and forgers discuss matters of right and wrong in a Talmudic study and prayer group, or 'minyan', led by a rabbi who's a fellow convict.

As the only prison in the federal system with a kosher deli, Otisville is the penitentiary of choice for white-collar Jewish offenders, many of whom secretly like the place. They've learned to game the system, so when the regime is toughened to punish a newly arrived celebrity convict who has upset the 45th president, they find devious ways to fight back.

Shadowy forces up the ante by trying to 'Epstein' – ie assassinate – the newcomer, and visiting poetry professor Deborah Liston ends up in dire peril when she sees too much. She has helped the minyan look into their souls. Will they now step up to save her?

Jonathan Stone brings the sensibility of Saul Bellow and Philip Roth to the post-truth era in a sharply comic novel that is also wise, profound and deeply moral.

*Erudite, trenchant and touching*
**Michael Arditti**

*There are crimes aplenty within the prison walls...but Stone is after something more diffuse and philosophical.* The Prison Minyan *occupies terrain few others will likely explore*
**New York Times**

*Rare is the book which is so delectable that, once you have finished it, you want immediately to read it all over again, but Jonathan Stone's glorious* The Prison Minyan *is just that… Stone's dry tones surely reach an apogee in this most cherishably Jewish of books*
**Jewish Chronicle**

If you have enjoyed *All God's Creatures*,
do please help us spread the word – by putting a review online;
by posting something on social media; or in the old-fashioned way
by simply telling your friends or family about it.

Book publishing is a very competitive business these days,
in a saturated market, and small independent publishers
such as ourselves are often crowded out by the big houses.
Support from readers like you can make all the difference
to a book's success.

Many thanks.

Dan Hiscocks
Founder, Eye Books